An Inmate's Daughter

An Inmate's Daughter

Jan Walker

with illustrations by Herb Leonhard

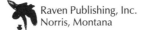

Raven Publishing, Inc.
Norris, Montana

An Inmate's Daughter © 2006 by Jan Walker

Published by Raven Publishing, Inc.
Norris, Montana
www.ravenpublishing.net

Cover art and illustrations © 2006 by Herb Leonhard
Book design by Jodi McPhee-Giddings
Printed in the United States of America

Library of Congress Cataloging-in-Publication Data

Walker, Jan (Janet D.)
    An inmate's daughter / Jan Walker ; with illustrations by Herb Leonhard.
        p. cm.
    Summary: During the summer between seventh and eighth grades, Jenna, her mother, and her little brother move in with her grandparents while her father is in a Washington State prison, but as Jenna tries to fit in and make friends it becomes increasingly difficult to comply with her mother's demands for secrecy.
    ISBN 0-9714161-9-2 (alk. paper)
    [1. Prisoners' families—Fiction. 2. Secrets—Fiction. 3. Peer pressure—Fiction. 4. Race awareness—Fiction. 5. Fathers—Fiction. 6. Grandparents—Fiction. 7. Washington (State)—Fiction.]
I. Leonhard, Herb, ill. II. Title.
PZ7.W15295In 2006
[Fic]—dc22

                                    2005035570

For Jo Nelson — 1946–2001
Writer, mentor, friend

A NOTE FROM THE AUTHOR

Dear Reader,

Jenna MacDonald is one of over two million children in the United States with a parent in prison or jail. When a parent is arrested, the first thing children need is a safe place to live. Jenna, her brother, and their mother are living with Jenna's grandparents in this story. The grandparents provide both security and love. That lets a thoughtful girl like Jenna sort through her life and how she feels about her dad, her mom, and the rules she's expected to follow.

Children also need to know their parents didn't abandon them. Many parents who are doing time were also using drugs and making other poor choices about their life style. Though it's not the children's fault, many think they are to blame. In this story, Jenna comes to understand that children are doing time, too.

Teachers, coaches, relatives and friends can all help children cope with the reality of prison by learning more about life inside. Most prisons offer a variety of education and treatment programs, jobs, recreation and hobby-shop opportunities. Most children understand school and work, and like to know what their parents are doing. Those who teach, counsel, or tend to men and women in prison or jail know every person has the ability to learn and change, and to make better choices for their future.

I taught parenting and family classes to hundreds of men like Jenna's dad, and to hundreds of women who were doing time. Those dads and moms loved their children. They worked hard to learn how to be better parents. I helped by listening to them and developing classes and programs that permitted them to reach out to their families. I hope this story, and others about children with parents doing time, gives you insight into their struggles.

—Jan Walker
December, 2005

Chapter One

On the first day of summer vacation between seventh and eighth grade, Jenna MacDonald did the dumbest thing ever. She tried to save a little girl from drowning. Most times, helping save someone would be a good thing. But not that time, at least not according to her mom.

"It's not *what*, Jenna, it's *where*," her mom said.

Where happened to be McNeil Island in Puget Sound, home of a prison and a wildlife sanctuary. Her dad lived in the prison. Jenna and her brother Zeke went to the island with their mom and grandpa and grandma for visiting.

Luckily, she did the dumbest thing ever *after* visiting her dad. If she'd done it before, Jenna's mom might have drowned her for drawing attention to the family. Keeping the fact of prison secret was a major rule.

Later, when the drowning girl and Jenna had both been plucked from the chilly waters of Puget Sound (those words came from the newspaper report) her mom kept asking *why*.

"Why, Jenna, when there were any number of adults right there?"

Jenna wanted to say "Duh." She'd fished Zeke out of the deep end of a swimming pool about a thousand times. Well, more than fifty. Their mom didn't know that. Jenna saved "Duh" for her journal, where she wrote about the "McNeil Island Incident." That's what corrections officers called it afterward.

"The incident grew out of the tensions of the day," she wrote. Those were her grandma's words. They sounded about right. The tensions began early on the morning of visiting.

"Get up, sleepyhead," Jenna's grandma called down the stairs to her basement bedroom. Her grandpa built the bedroom just for her before she and her mom and brother moved in. "You know what happens if we're late."

Jenna knew. They'd miss the prison visitors' bus to the McNeil Island boat, and there were no second chances. The visitors' bus picked them up at the state hospital. Grandpa Randall called it the loony bin to get Grandma's attention. It worked every time.

"Call it the psychiatric hospital and thank the powers that be you're not needing its services." Grandma slapped a piece of toast in front of Grandpa. "And eat some more. Heaven only knows when we'll see real food again."

Jenna opened her mouth to remind them they were leaving the island before noon. Before she could get a word out, Zeke slurped milk from his cereal bowl. He was four years younger than Jenna. Grandpa said Zeke's table manners didn't help matters. Grandpa wasn't exactly thrilled with the whole notion of visiting inside a prison. Jenna suspected he'd never liked her dad even before the fact of prison. She closed her mouth and tucked her lips between her teeth.

Zeke wiped his shirtsleeve across his mouth.

"Zeke, where's your napkin?" Grandma said. "Lynn, you've let this boy get out of hand. I tell you."

Lynn was Jenna and Zeke's mom. She had her hands full with her responsibilities. It wasn't easy for a woman with a husband behind bars.

"Zeke, you know better," their mother said. "Now hurry up and brush your teeth or we'll…"

Their mom let that dangle. She used to say, "Or we'll leave you behind." That's just what Zeke wanted. Two and a half hours in a prison visiting center bored him.

When they got settled in the car to drive to the bus depot, Jenna went into her journal mind. This is how we got to the bus depot. Lynn drove (she always used Lynn and Bernie, her mom and dad's names, in her journals) with Grandpa riding shotgun. That's what he called it even when Lynn said, "Please, Daddy, I've asked you not to say that." Lynn didn't like anything about guns, since Bernie MacDonald used one in the fight that sent him to prison. Jenna didn't like them, either. She could still hear the shot in her head, even though her mom said that was impossible since she'd been too young to remember.

When Lynn turned onto the freeway, Grandpa said, "Be faster to shoot on across west instead of going south."

Lynn said, "This is the way I always go. And I've asked you not to say 'shoot' all the time." Grandpa said, "You've lived here less than two months. That's not long enough to be always."

They'd moved into Grandpa and Grandma Randall's Tacoma home when the prison system moved Jenna's dad. At the old prison, called the Monroe Reformatory, visitors could drive up and park. Jenna and her mom and Zeke lived nearby in a trailer park. With a swimming pool. Other kids with a dad in prison lived there, too. Thanks to Zeke, who liked Jenna to rescue him from the deep end, she learned to be alert around water.

Grandpa and Grandma's house didn't have a pool, but it was in a good area. "No riff raff," Grandpa said. He painted the outside of the house Wedgwood blue (Grandma's favorite color) with white trim. Inside, Grandma had Wedgwood dishes hanging on the kitchen walls for decoration, not for food.

Jenna's mom and grandpa argued all the way to the bus depot. Jenna tuned out. Her journal could only handle so many Lynn and Grandpa spats. Only so many Lynn and Grandma spats, too, which started as soon as they parked.

"What's that?" Lynn said to Grandma. They were out of the car, walking to the bus.

"It's my handbag. What does it look like?"

"Mother, I told you. No handbags. What happened to the little zip bag I gave you?" Lynn shook her own clear plastic zip bag in her mother's face. It held her driver's license, cash for visiting room vending machines, a lipstick, a small hairbrush, and one car key.

"It's right in here." Grandma snapped open the clutch on her handbag.

"I told you the rules." Lynn grabbed Grandma's arm and spun her around.

Grandpa tapped his foot and held Zeke's shoulders while they waited. Zeke's feet kept moving, jumping, or shuffling.

A woman ahead of them tried to get four children into the visitors' bus. The child the woman carried wiggled. His little cloth shoe fell off. Jenna knew it was a boy because the shoe was blue. The woman pulled another boy along by the hand. He stepped on the shoe. Two girls with the woman held hands and skipped.

The woman said, "One of you girls pick up the baby's shoe and then get your behinds up them steps." The girls picked up the shoe with their held hands. They giggled.

"What's with that, anyway?" Grandpa asked. "One girl white, one black, and the boy an Indian?"

Grandma caught up with them. "Shh, the whole county can hear you. I think the boy's Asian."

"They're a mixed family," Jenna said and went back into her thoughts. She'd been at Howard Middle School for eight weeks. So far she didn't have even one friend, and now it was summer break. And almost her thirteenth birthday. She wanted to become a member of the Snoops, a mixed group. Sara, one of the four leaders, said, "We're international. We're looking for a Mexican member."

"Sara means Hispanic," Dori said. "Because of her boyfriend."

Then Sara whispered to Dori, "Maybe Jenna's, like, Hispanic. Her hair and eyes are black. And her skin's, like, tan all the time."

The Snoops always whispered loud enough to be overheard when they wanted to make outsiders jealous. They kept their name secret. Jenna called them the Snoops after they followed her home from school to rate her for their club. So far she didn't rate high enough to suit the leaders, Lori and Kara, Dori and Sara, whose real names were Lorraine, Karen, Doris, and Sarah with an *h*. Snoops names could have only four letters. It was one of their rules.

Jenna came back from her thoughts about the Snoops when her grandpa said, "Mother's Indian. That's why I made the call the boy's Indian." Grandpa meant Native American. Jenna was part Native American and zero Hispanic.

"Will you both please shut up," Lynn said in her I-mean-it voice.

They all stayed quiet on the short winding bus ride to the waterfront. They stayed quiet while they walked across the railroad tracks. Then Zeke ran ahead and climbed on the dock railing and had to be pulled down. Jenna tried to walk by herself, while her mom, grandma, and grandpa all scolded Zeke.

They entered the building through the door with

warnings over it. The building belonged to the Department of Corrections. They called the prison the McNeil Island Corrections Center. Inside the building, Jenna and Zeke and their mom lined up behind the locked door on their right. Grandma stuck with them. Grandpa headed for the door on the left—the door without a line.

A black man in a blue corrections officer uniform yelled, "Hey, you in the gray jacket. You gotta use this door over here." He had a deep voice. Everyone looked at Grandpa.

Jenna's mom said, "Daddy," in her I've-about-had-it voice. Jenna grabbed her grandpa's hand and held it while they waited for their turn. Jenna's mom and grandma put their clear plastic bags on the tray for inspection. They all lined up to go through the metal detector. Grandpa had to take off his belt and shoes. He wasn't exactly thrilled about that. Jenna squeezed his hand.

She squeezed tighter when the officer in charge of the dock shouted, "Inmate visitors stand back. Let island residents and staff board first."

"I tell you," Grandma said.

"I know, Grandma," Zeke said. "They won't let you walk around on the boat, either. And when it gets to the dock and they tie it up, you have to stay seated until all the important people get off."

"We're important," Grandpa Randall said. "Important enough to pay taxes." According to Grandpa, taxes kept inmates clothed and fed.

"Daddy, just hush, please." Lynn's voice reached her exasperated level. Jenna recognized it. Their mom used "hush" with Zeke about a hundred times a day. Well, five at least.

It took the boat twenty minutes to cross Puget Sound to McNeil Island. Grandpa Randall stayed quiet all the way across and all the way up the ramp. He stayed quiet right up until he realized the long, empty van waiting on the island dock wasn't there to give visitors rides.

"What's it for, then?"

"It drives behind us to keep us in line," Zeke said. And then zigzagged out of line just for fun.

The boy that was either Indian or Asian followed Zeke. The woman said something to the two girls. They pulled him back.

"Seems to me they could give that woman with the four little ones a ride," Grandpa said.

"Mother," Lynn said, "can you please hush daddy before we all get sent back to the other side?"

Jenna's journal mind had filled with spats and rules. She stared at the backs of people walking toward the prison. It kept her eyes off the fence topped with razor wire. And the tower. Where a guard had a gun. Aimed right at them. She couldn't see the guard or the gun, but she knew it was there.

Zeke liked the fence. "See those Slinky wires, Grandpa? On top of the fence? There's a million-trillion-zillion razors on the Slinky to slice you to pieces, and your blood drips out and…"

"Zeke, shut up." Their mom grabbed Zeke's arm and jerked it.

"Would you look at that," Grandpa said. "Deer browsing along the hillside right up close to the fence. Who'd a thunk it?"

"Thunk, thunk." Zeke bopped his head. He tried to go into a pretend shooter's crouch, but their mom jerked his arm again, and he said, "Ouch, Mom," like the words had ten syllables each.

Jenna moved closer to the dock rails. Ducks bobbed along on the waves of the silvery water. Maybe her mom wouldn't notice. She'd be busy with Zeke, and Jenna could slip between other visitors. She kept her eyes on the water when they turned the bend and started up the sidewalk and walked toward the gate.

Grandpa said to Grandma, "This isn't my idea of how to spend my Saturday. Mowing the lawn beats the heck out of this."

"Oh, for Pete's sake, it's for your daughter and your grandchildren." Lots of Grandma's comments included Pete. It was just a saying, according to her grandma. She didn't even know anyone named Pete.

Most of the ducks were ordinary brownish-black, but one had a white circle on its head. Jenna made a mental note to ask her dad what it was called. He used to hunt ducks with his shotgun and deer with his rifle. Her mom said he'd been out hunting the night he got into that fight. The fight where one man died, and one got shot in the leg. Her dad walked with a limp.

He was three-fourths Canadian Indian and smart about wildlife and stuff. He was one-fourth mixed-up by adoption, so the Indian part was what mattered most.

That made Jenna three-eighths Indian. Or Native American, depending on who you talked to. The Snoops didn't have one of those, either. They weren't exactly looking for one.

Like it even mattered. She was sure none of the Snoops wanted a member whose dad was in prison for murder.

Chapter Two

Jenna got the first hug from her dad when they all got together at a table in the visitors' room. A square table for four, with two extra chairs. She knew he'd meant to hug Zeke first, but Zeke plopped right down. Tripped and plopped and broke the rule about noise just like that. Grandma and Grandpa said, "Shh," and their mom jerked Zeke's arm to sit him up straight in the chair. Their dad said, "Easy, Sport."

Zeke shrugged loose from their mom's grasp. "I'm not Sport. I'm Zeke." His feet kicked out, on accident he said, and sent a chair scraping across the floor.

Jenna watched a woman officer come their way and missed seeing the important hug. The one between her dad and mom. She usually watched her dad, who kissed and hugged her mom with his eyes closed. Sometimes when he opened them they were wet, but just a little. Her mom always looked at her feet after the kiss and hug. Like her shoes needed checking. Jenna wanted to know if her mom and dad were still in love.

The officer's badge said C/O Santos. C/O stood for correctional officer. She had black hair and eyes. If she attended Howard Middle, the Snoops would invite her to join their group. She was Mexican or Hispanic or whatever and pretty.

"How you folks doing?" C/O Santos said.

"We're fine, thanks," Jenna's dad said. When the officer moved on he said, "Lynn, you cannot put your hands on the kids that way."

"What way? I was just straightening him up in his chair."

Zeke wiggled, which made his chair rock, which made all four adults say his name at once. Then Grandma and Grandpa asked questions like, "How's it going?" Jenna tuned out after that and watched the C/O's watch the room. They sat on a stage with a low wall across the front. She'd stopped by the stage steps and peeked the last time they visited. There was a big desk, telephones, and stacks of paper. It looked boring—like school got boring. Sit at a desk and wait for something to happen. Finally, their mom gave Zeke some money so he could buy a treat from the vending machines.

When it was Jenna's turn to talk to her dad, he asked if she had any new friends. She shrugged and said, "Sort of." So he said, "Tell me about them." Her mom said that came from the psychology degree he got through some prison program. *Tell me about this. Tell me about that. Bernie never talked like that before.*

Anyway, Jenna liked talking to her dad, so she told him about the Snoops. He laughed about their name.

Then her dad got real serious. She could tell by his eyes. They got smaller, and wrinkles showed at the corners.

"What do you think would happen if you told those girls the truth? That your dad's in prison?" Her dad kept his voice low, almost a whisper.

Jenna shrugged. "I'm not allowed to tell. Mom and Grandma both said." Then her mouth started running. That's what her mom called it. "It was easier before, when you were at the reformatory, because my friend Crystal's dad was in prison. Remember? And other kids in the trailer park had dads there, too. And kids at school knew already, and it didn't matter so much."

"It sounds like you're feeling a little sad and a little lonely for your friends."

Jenna nodded, just a little nod, and moved her head enough to see what her mom and grandparents were doing. Grandpa had his arms folded across his chest. Her mom and grandma were whispering, probably about some man's crime. Or some woman's clothes. If her mom had heard her dad, she'd say something about how her dad talked to her. *It sounds like you're feeling sad. Who are you to talk about feelings, Bernie MacDonald?*

And then Jenna asked the dumb question. The whiny one. "When do you get to come home?" She didn't mean to ask. She'd promised herself she wouldn't. She knew the answer. Three more years. But prison rules changed all the time, and her dad had a clean record. That meant he didn't have infractions from breaking the rules. He never lost any good time and never got sent to the hole.

She knew all about good time. The prison took time

off a sentence for good behavior. She didn't know much about the hole because her dad never went there. He said men in the hole stayed in a small room all alone for twenty-three out of twenty-four hours. They got out one hour for a shower and some exercise.

Her dad leaned close to her. His dark eyes looked sad. Maybe hers did, too, they were so much like his. His skin was darker than hers; he spent all the time he could outside.

"I'll be home before you graduate from high school. You hold onto that, Jenna. I'm going to be at your graduation. And another thing. I know it's hard to move away from friends. I had a good friend at the reformatory. Sometimes it feels lonely here without him to talk to. It's important to have someone to talk to about feelings."

Lonely. That's how she felt, even with Grandma and Grandpa and her mom and Zeke. She knew her mom felt that way, too. She thought about that: her mom feeling lonely but acting mad. Jenna lowered her eyes so her dad wouldn't see them. She studied some tickets he'd put on the table. Photo chits. Her dad had to buy them ahead of the visit.

When they got the signal that it was their turn for pictures, they clumped together in front of a big plant and smiled. Grandma made Grandpa unfold his arms. She held Zeke in front of her to keep him still. Jenna stood in front of her grandpa and snuck one of her hands into his. Lynn stood in front of Bernie. Jenna liked to think of them that way. Lynn and Bernie. A married couple.

The photographer gave Jenna's dad the picture, a Polaroid. Her dad passed it on to Grandma, who said she'd hang it right in the middle of the refrigerator door. Then her dad gave the photographer the other ticket.

"Just my daughter and me, for her birthday. It's next week. She'll be thirteen."

"A young lady," the photographer said.

Jenna didn't know what to do with her arms. Her dad put one hand on her shoulder. She ended up with her arms behind her back. Her mom didn't like the picture.

"Neither one of you smiled right. You both look like you lost your last friend."

That about covered it, Jenna thought. It was Zeke's turn to talk to their dad, but he'd wandered over to the children's play area, even though it was for younger kids. Grandpa kept looking at his watch. Grandma said, "I tell you" about ten times. She must have seen some couples sneaking kisses on the lips. Kisses and hugs were permitted only for hello and goodbye, and not at all during the visit. It was a very important rule. Breaking it could mean no more visits forever, or at least for a very long time.

Her dad gave out hugs again when they got up to leave. He hugged her mom last and held on to her hand when she started to walk away. Jenna's journal eyes watched Lynn pull her hand from Bernie's. Sometimes kids at school did that, but without the scrunched eyebrows that meant Lynn was about to lose it. Grandpa pushed at Grandma's back like he did when he wanted her to hurry.

Hurry didn't exactly happen outside Visiting. They

had to line up to check out of the building and line up outside in the holding pen for the gate to open. That's what it looked like to Jenna—a holding pen for cattle just like she'd seen in a film at school. Then they had to walk in line down the sidewalk to the dock. That was the rule.

Zeke found parts of clamshells that seagulls had dropped on the walk and stomped on them. Jenna's dad told her the gulls dropped them to crack the shell so they could eat the clam. Zeke found a big one that made a loud sound when he stomped.

"Stop it, Zeke, right this minute. I mean it," their mom said.

Zeke crunched one more shell, then slipped in between Grandma and Grandpa. Jenna looked for the duck with the white circle. She'd forgotten to ask her dad about it, but that meant she had something to write about to him. The tide was low. Blue herons stood in the water watching the people go by. Her dad had told her they were called great blue herons and drew a picture of one in flight. Grandpa said with a little head like that, he was surprised the bird had enough brains to get that huge body in the air.

"It's their instinct, Grandpa. Dad says it's innate."

At the same time, Zeke said, "Bird-brain, bird-brain."

Jenna ignored him. She was thinking about what her dad might be sending for her birthday. He said he'd made something. "Watch for your birthday package," he'd said. She hoped he'd made some more pictures for her collection. He sketched and did watercolors and block prints of wild things. Bears and wolves and eagles. And a hummingbird. He made her a set of stationery with hummingbirds. Her mom said it was just plain old copy paper. Like the art didn't count because her dad couldn't get better paper.

Her mom wasn't always like that. She was just tired of the whole thing. Meaning prison and visiting and not enough money. She'd gone back to school now that they lived with Grandpa and Grandma. She enrolled in a paralegal program to learn more about the law. But it wasn't easy because she still had to work.

The woman with the four kids was right in front of them on the sidewalk. She'd sat with two men in Visiting, one black and one like Jenna's dad. More or less white. The girls swung their hands and jumped over cracks in the sidewalk. "Stop it, girls. Can't you just walk?" the woman said. They stopped jumping but kept swinging their hands and giggling.

The low tide made the ramp down to the float steep. "Watch your step, now," an officer said over and over. Jenna thought he or someone would help the woman. No one helped. The woman clutched the wiggling baby in one arm and held onto the boy's hand. "You two stay right behind me now, you hear?" she said to the girls. "Hold onto them rails." The woman needed to work on her grammar.

The girls couldn't reach the top rail. They moved their hands from one upright to the next and put the toes of their shoes right up against each cross rib on the ramp. The boy caught hold of an upright and clung. The woman pulled. One blue cloth shoe fell out of the baby's blanket and drifted down to the float.

"Get that shoe," the woman said to the girls before they even reached the bottom of the ramp. Just as the girls were ready to pick it up, a breeze scooted it closer to the edge opposite where the boat was tied. Opposite the way they were allowed to walk. The girls darted after it.

Someone yelled, "Hey, get back in line."

The white girl grabbed the little shoe. The black girl tripped over the white girl's foot and tumbled head first into the silvery water. The woman screamed.

Jenna's mom and grandma screamed. Her grandpa said, "Someone help her."

An officer said, "Oh, shit."

And that's when Jenna did the dumbest thing ever. She should have known better now that she was almost thirteen. But she didn't stop to think about how her actions would affect her mom's life. She ran to the float edge and jumped in after the girl. Just like she'd jumped into the pool at the trailer park where they used to live. Zeke couldn't swim. He thought being rescued was a game.

Jenna heard her grandma say, "I tell you." Then water filled her ears.

Chapter Three

The water was cold and dark, not at all like the pool at the trailer park where they used to live. She saw the girl's dress and swung her arms out and pulled her knees up to put on her brakes. The girl's arms and legs were moving but not the right way. Her dress floated up, and her mouth was open. Jenna grabbed for an arm and caught the dress. The girl thrashed and kicked. *Close your mouth!* Jenna tried her hardest to send a mind message. Her hand grabbed the girl's arm. It was a tiny arm, but strong. It tugged and fought Jenna, and a foot kicked her. Jenna used her free hand to paddle and pull upward and kicked so hard she kicked the girl's foot.

Jenna felt something wrap around her middle. An octopus. She should have known something like that would happen. Now she had to fight it and the girl. The octopus grabbed the girl, too. It squeezed Jenna's held breath out of her and made her chest ache. She put all her strength into twisting. The octopus squeezed harder. At least they were floating up, not down.

Water got in Jenna's mouth. Saltwater with an icky taste. She blew out and twisted, and the octopus turned into a man. With big arms. And one hand that touched too close to her chest where no one was allowed to touch her. Before she could do anything about that, daylight cut right into her eyes. Cold air rolled over every part of her body. Screams pushed right through her ears into the middle of her head. The same screams she'd heard before she jumped in. Her mom's screams and the woman's screams and then one loud, deep, I-mean-it voice.

"Board the boat now! Get on board. That's an order."

Jenna saw blue uniforms everywhere. She couldn't get to her mom or grandparents. Goosebumps covered her skin. Water squished in her shoes. If they were ruined, her mom would have a fit. She'd have to stuff the toes with newspaper until they dried out.

A siren whined. It sounded a lot like Zeke when he didn't get his way. A man in regular clothes with a black bag in his hand ran down the ramp, steep as it was. One blue uniform dripped on the float. The octopus. Jenna giggled. A shiver rolled up from her legs to her head, and back down. Voices on top of voices. Her grandpa's gray jacket around her. His face close to hers. Tears on his cheeks. Two more men ran down the ramp. They had blankets. They wrapped one around her and two around the little girl. Blue uniforms got in the way. Jenna couldn't tell if the girl was breathing.

The I-mean-it voice bellowed, "Board the boat."

Jenna's grandpa said, "I'm her grandfather, and I'll board the boat when she does."

...the octopus turned into a man.

Jenna's heart pounded. Her chest ached from holding her breath. Her fingers tingled, and her middle felt like that arm still held it. Her teeth jumped into each other when she opened her mouth, but she had to tell somebody about the girl having her mouth open. "She was drinking the water. The little girl. I didn't know how to make her close her mouth."

Serious shaking took control of Jenna's body. Her arms jerked, and her legs felt like they'd gone to sleep and couldn't hold her up. Her grandpa held onto her like he knew she was wobbly. Or maybe he just held on like he loved her.

The I-mean-it voice bellowed, "Strip them kids. Get them out of those wet clothes. We don't need them catchin' pneumonia on state time."

A black woman officer popped out of nowhere and wrapped another blanket around Jenna. Wrapped it right over her head and around her face. "They're talking trash. Ain't nobody going to be doing any stripping out here." She lifted Jenna into her arms and cradled her like a baby. "You did fine. You're a hero. Come on now. You too Grandpa; you're coming with me. We're going up to the wheelhouse to see the captain. Ain't nobody going to be takin' off your clothes up there, either."

"The little girl…" Jenna stretched to see over the woman's shoulder.

"She's going to be just fine."

Behind them, Jenna heard a moan, then uhh, uhh, uhh.

"Hear that, girl?" the officer said. "She's tossing out the seawater right now. Wonder if she swallowed any of those little fish that swim around the float."

The woman officer carried Jenna right past her mom.

"Jenna," her mom yelled. "That was the dumbest thing you ever did." At the same time, Grandma called, "Jenna? Jenna!" A man sat between them. Jenna heard him say, "Stay seated."

Her mom stayed seated, but she got in the last word. "Jenna's almost thirteen. She should know better."

The officer carried Jenna up the stairs she'd been told never to climb and around seats that looked like the ones downstairs. Gray and hard. The officer turned sideways to get through a door onto the deck and then through another door. The captain's wheelhouse. The captain wore a white shirt, navy pants, and a proper captain's hat. Orange life vests covered most of the floor. When the woman kneeled down to lay Jenna on the life vests, her knees creaked.

"Just never you mind that noise; that's my knees popping some fat bubbles. Grandpa, you sit right there. The captain wants to ask you some questions. Jenna? That's you, right? We want you to relax on this here sad excuse for a bed. Someone's going to come along any minute now and take your blood pressure. Then, if you're doing okay, the captain has some questions for you, too."

The woman pushed Jenna's hair back from her face with one hand. She had long red fingernails and the biggest diamond Jenna had ever seen. Plus other rings. She dabbed Jenna's face with a towel and took her wrist to check her pulse all at once. Her name badge said C/O Hooper, and her skin was rosy brown—not black at all.

"My mom's going to be mad about my shoes."

"Pay no mind to your shoes, girl. You've got some new shoes coming. Some of us can see to that. Right Sarge?"

Jenna looked up at the man who stood outside the doorway. His skin was like her dad's. Not white, not black, just tan. Something about him reminded her of her dad. It wasn't his height; he had to duck to get inside, which meant he was taller. It was something in his face.

"I'm Sergeant Kanahele." He squatted down beside her, took her hand in his big one, and shook it. "I'm the one who gets to ask the official questions after a P/A sees you. We'll bring your mother upstairs when the P/A gets here."

"P/A stands for physician's assistant," Officer Hooper said. "He's like a doctor."

Jenna nodded and looked at the sergeant. "Are you a Native American?" She hadn't meant to ask, but it squirted right out like her brain lost its brakes in the cold water. Which meant it was on her mind because of the Snoops. Who might think a Native American was okay for their club if they heard what the black officer said. You're a hero. She forgot all about her mom for a minute or two.

"Native Hawaiian," the sergeant said, "which might be close to the same thing."

Then he said the most important thing of all.

"I understand you're Bernie MacDonald's daughter.

I've met him. He's a good man. He's going to swell right up with pride when he hears about this."

Jenna started to smile, but her mom's face appeared behind the sergeant, and her mom's words ruined the whole thing. Her words and her eyes, which were pale blue and hard as ice. Except ice would melt.

"Well, I hope to God you don't intend to broadcast it. Jenna, do you hear me? This is not a matter to be discussed outside the family. Ever. That's the rule."

Chapter Four

It turned out her mom's rule wouldn't start until later. Jenna had to tell the whole thing to Sergeant Kanahele and the guy who acted like a doctor but was only an assistant. And to C/O Hooper, who rubbed Jenna's arms and legs with a towel. She'd sneak a hand inside the blankets, lift out an arm, rub, put it back, and lift out the other.

The sergeant asked Grandpa Randall all sorts of questions, which Grandpa answered in his serious voice. Then the sergeant said the thing that Jenna could tell got her grandpa going. When things made him mad, he'd say, "Don't get me going."

The sergeant said, "You were the one closest to your granddaughter, Mr. Randall. Right? You saw the whole thing?"

Grandpa Randall's upper lip twitched before words came out, and his neck and face got dark red. "She squirted right past me. You think I just stood by and let my

Jenna jump in the drink? You think I didn't try to grab hold of her?"

The sergeant said, "No sir, that's not what I think. What I think is you were shocked just like a whole lot of other folk. I'm just gathering information. Kind of like a traffic report."

Grandpa Randall nodded then.

C/O Hooper said, "You doin' okay here, Mr. Randall?"

"Well enough, all things considered."

Jenna's mom said, "I was busy seeing to my son. He's hyperactive. He's a handful." That meant it wasn't her fault that Jenna squirted past Grandpa.

Grandpa Randall said, "None of this would have happened if someone had given that woman with all those kids a hand. Four little ones like that, and you use one of your officers—who's getting paid with tax dollars by the way—you use one of your officers to drive a van, length of a city bus, along behind us and leave a woman burdened like that to walk. You ought to be ashamed."

"Daddy, it's a rule," Jenna's mom said.

"Oh, hang the rules, Lynnie."

Jenna liked that. *Hang the rules.* She'd like to hang them. She'd like to tell someone about her dad and prison and how it felt to be an inmate's daughter. Jenna expected her grandpa to say the rest. The swear word he used as an adjective, and Grandma said, "Darn works just as well." But he didn't; he just fixed his look on Lynn, who gave in and looked at her shoes.

At the same time the captain talked on a phone. It was hard to hear what he said with the sergeant asking her questions. "What did you see? Why did you jump in so fast when there were uniforms around?" That part bothered him, Jenna could tell.

"I didn't think; I just reacted," she said.

"Vitals all good, lungs clear, temp about right," the P/A said.

While the others were saying, "Good, good," Jenna asked to sit up, but they all told her she needed to rest, and then they talked across her.

Sergeant Kanahele said, "What happened to the other gurney?"

The P/A said, "Mix-up. Somebody misunderstood; younger one got the gurney. Duty officer ordered the captain to get this tub untied and across the big pond."

All the way across to Steilacoom, the mainland town where the visitors' bus waited, Jenna's mom had that look on her face—the worried look where her eyebrows got close together, and her lips got tucked between her teeth. The look stayed in place until the boat slowed down, and the captain got off the phone.

"What exactly do you plan to do with this information?" Jenna's mom asked.

Sergeant Kanahele rubbed a hand across his face. "Incident report first. That's what I'm going to be working on. Every one of us will do a write-up." His hand swept the air. "Captain, C/O Hooper, P/A Munger, me."

"Lot of paper be used up over this, girl." C/O Hooper

squeezed Jenna's hand, which she'd fished out of the blanket.

"Then an investigation. Sorry, ma'am, uh, Ms. MacDonald, but there will likely be calls from Olympia. From headquarters. DOC...uh, Department of Corrections information officer. I need your address and phone number." He waited a beat, then said, "I know we have them on file on your visitor's form, but I'd like to record them here. If you don't mind."

Jenna's mom fixed the sergeant with her narrowed-eye stare. "Sergeant, you hear me and you hear me good. Do not let your information officer or anyone else tell any of this to the news people.

Jenna liked how the sergeant handled that. He put a hand on Jenna's mom's arm and gave her a nice smile.

"Trust me, ma'am, the department will not want this in the news. Your best bet—and I'm serious as a heart attack about this—it's best you work with the department's information officer. The investigation will go on until someone a whole lot higher than me says it's closed."

Jenna's mom leaned in toward the sergeant. "Fine. We'll talk with the information officer. You just see to it that no one else talks. You hear?"

C/O Hooper kind of groaned, and Sergeant Kanahele closed his eyes for a few seconds. Jenna thought he must be doing all sorts of inside things to keep from laughing.

"Ma'am, there's over a hundred passengers aboard this boat. Staff and visitors."

"Hundred and thirty-eight," the captain said. Then he

pushed a button and said, "Attention. May I have your attention? We have two ambulances on the dock and two passengers aboard who need to be transported. Please remain seated until you hear the all-clear bell. I repeat. ALL passengers remain seated."

Next thing, while Jenna's mom was arguing about ambulances, and her grandpa was saying, "Now, Lynnie, they've been explaining," and C/O Hooper was patting her arm through the blankets, two guys showed up with a bed on wheels.

"Okay, who's the lucky one gets the ride?"

Chapter Five

Jenna waited in the ambulance on the bed with wheels that popped down and up. One guy, who said he was a medic, stuck a needle in her arm. "Ouch," she said. Her eyes climbed from her arm up the tube to a clear plastic bag.

"Glucose," the medic said. "Sugar water. Hold your arm still."

The medic held onto her arm so she couldn't have moved it if she'd wanted. The other ambulance guy—the driver—tried to get Jenna's mom in the back, too, so they could leave. Jenna heard a whoop-whoop from the other ambulance, the one with the little girl. She lifted her head and went into her journal mind. Uniforms and badges: Steilacoom Police, Pierce County Sheriff, Washington State Patrol, McNeil Island Corrections Officers, one with his hands on Zeke's shoulders.

"Just a *minute*," Lynn said, "I've got to get things sorted out."

"Stand still, son," the officer said to Zeke.

"Daddy, you drive but watch your tailgating and wide turns. Mother, you hold on to Zeke. I'll call you as soon I know what they're doing with Jenna. Find her some dry clothes and bring them to the hospital. Remember socks and shoes. And underwear. Mother, are you listening?"

"Lynn, I've been dressing myself for almost seventy years now, you think I'd forget undergarments?"

Zeke went into his chant. "What's under there? Under where? Underwear."

Jenna groaned. The guy with her patted her arm, which he'd been holding still because of the needle. He'd wrapped her in a blue blanket and put a thing like a bonnet over her head and warm things on her legs and feet. She could almost fall asleep, if her mom ever got things sorted out.

A deep voice shouted, "All right, let's get things rolling here. There's a boat full of people to offload. This here's taking longer than molasses in January." Someone helped Lynn into the ambulance. A train whistled, the ambulance doors closed, the train whistled again just ahead of the clang-clang of barricades lowering to block the tracks.

Jenna closed her eyes and waited for the lecture. She thought about molasses in January. She'd add that to the pages of Grandma and Grandpa sayings in her journal. Jenna's mom said, "Why? That's all I want to know."

The medic said, "Hush, now." Jenna's mom stayed quiet after that. The ambulance rocked as the train rumbled past. Jenna squeezed her eyes tighter when they bounced over the tracks, tilted through turns, climbed and descended hills. They slowed now and then but never stopped.

The medic held her arm with the needle. "Going through a red light. There. Made it. Won't be long now."

When Jenna opened her eyes she saw her mom slumped over, elbows on knees, face down in her hands. Jenna wanted to remind her mom about the sit-up-straight rule. The medic smiled like he knew her thoughts.

The ambulance stopped, the back door opened, and the driver helped Jenna's mom get out. Then both medics pulled Jenna's bed out, and the wheels popped down, and away she went, backward so she never saw where she was going, only where she'd been. They backed her through swinging doors and up alongside a bed. She saw three other beds and curtain walls and heard voices. One voice belonged to a nurse who whipped curtains around Jenna. It sounded like a very long zipper being pulled. They were alone—the nurse and Jenna.

"We're going to get you out of those wet clothes and into a gown. Doctor will be along soon."

Before Jenna could answer, the blue blanket and head thing and leg warmers were gone. Her clothes were pulled up and over and down and off, and a gown with teddy bears stretched from her chin to her ankles. Blankets got tucked around her. The curtains zipped again. The nurse said, "One, two, three," and Jenna sailed off one bed and onto the other.

The medic who'd ridden with her said, "You take care now." The driver saluted, and the prison blanket and ambulance warmers rode away in a heap.

Jenna watched her mom pace, even after the nurse told her to bring a chair. Her mom walked around the bed, out into the corridor, and back in again. Jenna closed her eyes and waited for the explosion. She wished her mom would hit her a couple times and yell and get it over with.

She must have dozed off, because the next thing she knew, the doctor was there—a woman doctor—asking questions. Jenna told the whole story again and answered that she felt fine—no headache, no chest ache. The doctor listened all over her front and back with the stethoscope and looked in her eyes and ears and mouth.

The doctor said, "Everything looks good. You can get dressed."

Grandma Randall came in through the curtain with a brown bag and Jenna's old running shoes that were a bit too small. She felt Jenna's forehead with the back of her hand and looked in her eyes like she was a doctor, too.

"Where's my mom?"

"Checking you out. We'll meet her in the lobby."

Her mom stayed quiet all the way to Grandma Randall's car and all the way out of the parking lot. Then she turned around in the passenger seat and gave Jenna her narrowed-eyes look. "What…ever…possessed you?"

Grandma said, "Now Lynn…"

"Don't you 'Now Lynn' me, Mother. Do you realize…"

Jenna slumped into a corner of the back seat and stared out the side window while her grandma and mom argued about the proper time and place, and then they were home, parked on the street in front of the Wedgwood blue house with white trim and white wicker furniture on the big front porch. "Pretty as a picture," Grandma said about the house.

Jenna went up the steps, across the porch, through the door and the living room and then the kitchen and straight downstairs to her basement bedroom. She flopped on her bed and wondered if Grandma regretted having them move in. They were like a bad chapter in a good book. That was a saying, but not from Grandma. Jenna stayed on her bed, face down, until Grandma called her for dinner.

They all stuck to what Grandpa called the serious business of eating. Grandma reminded Zeke about his manners twice and made the "eat your vegetables" speech once. Jenna's stomach growled from hunger, but she remembered her manners. Grandma was clearing the table for dessert before Mom even looked at Jenna. It was her look that came before serious punishment.

"Jenna, I just want to know why."

Grandma turned off the water but stayed by the sink.

Grandpa and Zeke looked at Jenna and then at the places where their plates had been.

Jenna looked at her mom. It was one of those questions that had only wrong answers.

"Why, when there were people around...any number

of people who are supposed to be responsible for visitors. Why did you run past them and jump in? That's all I want to know. Just what possessed you to do that?"

Zeke's chair rocked, and he slurped in drool that was about to drip. "Probably cuz she jumped into the pool to save me all the time. Cuz I can't swim, 'member, Mom?"

Their mom's head turned from Jenna to Zeke. A slow turn, like the hinges were rusty. Her mouth opened, but no words came.

"The trailer park pool," Zeke said. "Where we lived before."

Jenna felt her dinner jump around in her stomach. Her eyes went closed. The rule about Zeke was stay-out-of-the-deep-end. She'd intended to keep saying she didn't know what possessed her, but Zeke blew that. He gave them up. Now they were both in trouble.

Grandma turned the water back on and rattled dishes, but she kept her ears open. Jenna could tell.

Zeke wiggled so hard the chair moved a foot. "See, it's like I learned on the science channel about spontaneous combustion. I fall in, and Jenna has a spontaneous combustion."

"Reaction. You mean spontaneous reaction, Zeke." Grandpa had a hand on the back of Zeke's chair. "Spontaneous combustion is what your mom's about to do. If she's not careful, she'll explode and burn."

Jenna knew he was trying to bring a lighter note to things. That was another one of his sayings. It turned out one journal page for each grandparent's sayings wasn't going to be enough.

After that, it all came out. The babysitter, who their mom paid good money, didn't watch them because she had a boyfriend. The end of baby sitters when Zeke turned six because he was in school all day and Jenna could see to him after school. Since that worked out okay, as far as their mom knew, Jenna saw to him during vacations, too.

"When she was only ten?" Grandma left the sink with water running right down the drain. Water ran down Grandma's arms, too, and dripped onto the floor, and her face had a look that Jenna could describe as sick. "Lynn? You left her in charge of Zeke with all his problems when she was only ten?"

"Mother, you don't have a clue. You don't know what it's like. None of you know what it's like to be married to a man in prison. The man doesn't help in any way, especially not with money. You don't know..." Tears rolled down Lynn's face.

Grandpa looked at Grandma, then at Lynn. "Seems to me there's laws about leaving kids unsupervised."

"They knew the rules, Daddy. Zeke was not allowed to go beyond the three feet part of the pool." Lynn slapped away the tears and glared at Jenna.

"There's rules and there's laws, Lynnie. Kids maybe broke a rule, but it looks to me like you broke a law." Grandpa's upper lip twitched. Red scalp showed right through his white hair.

"Well, maybe that comes with being married to a criminal. The wife gets treated like a criminal, too, when she didn't do anything. It's a vicious circle." Lynn pushed away from the table so hard her chair fell over.

Zeke made his hands into claws and scratched the air. "Vicious. Rrr-aaah-err."

Grandma and Grandpa both said, "Zeke!" but their eyes were on Lynn, who was sobbing and running up the stairs.

"I tell you," Grandma said.

"I know, Grandma," Jenna said. "Mom has her hands full."

Chapter Six

Jenna tiptoed around the kitchen and shushed Zeke, who did sound effects along with the TV. It was early Sunday morning. Grandpa Randall wandered into the kitchen in his pajamas.

"Don't you two know it's too early for decent folks to be out of bed? What are you doing up?"

Jenna turned the TV down another notch and put a finger over her lips for Zeke to see. "Watching cartoons, Grandpa. We'll be quiet."

Their grandpa shook his head and headed back to bed. Maybe he didn't know she'd outgrown cartoons years ago. She was sure he didn't understand how hyper Zeke got after a visit to their dad. This morning, Zeke was more wired than ever, which was Jenna's fault for squirting past her grandpa and jumping into the drink.

Their dad told Jenna and her mom what happened to hyper children like Zeke.

"Visiting a separated parent stirs up all sorts of behavior. It takes a day or two to get back to normal."

Their dad said it was in a book about parenting and child development. He didn't understand that Zeke's normal wasn't all that good.

Jenna wrote what her dad said in her journal with quotes and his name. After it, she wrote her mom's response.

"Bernie MacDonald, child psychologist."

The words didn't look anything like they'd sounded, so she had to write how her mom scrunched up her face and almost spit. Later, when Jenna read back through her journal, she added another word to describe her mom. Sarcastic. Which meant their mom was angry, too. Jenna knew that much about sarcasm.

"I'll make us some French toast, Zeke, and heat Grandma's homemade syrup if you just promise to keep the volume down. The TV's and yours." Jenna squatted in front of him and wrapped one of Grandma's Afghans around him so his arms were tucked in. Her dad told her mom to try that.

While she was talking about French toast, Zeke was saying, "Zzzrooooom," and then something that sounded like an oink, but he did it sort of quietly and gave her his twinkle-eyed grin. She patted his arm through the blanket, like the woman officer had done to her on the boat, and touched a finger to her lips again. Then she washed up, got out eggs and milk and a bowl and beater, and plugged in Grandma's electric frying pan. Zeke was eating his third piece of French toast swimming in syrup when their grandma came into the kitchen. She had on a soft pink bathrobe. Her gray curls were flat against her head, and there were sleep creases on her face.

"What on earth is going on out here?"

Jenna couldn't tell if their grandma was upset or just surprised. "I just fixed Zeke's breakfast, Grandma. I'll clean up the mess. I promise."

"I'm not worried about the mess. Since when do you fix Zeke's breakfast?" Their grandma went to the cupboard where she kept coffee beans and pulled them out.

"Since for a long time, but only special ones on Sundays after Mom goes out on Saturday night. Which she mostly does after we've visited Dad."

Jenna flipped a piece of bread. It was a perfect golden brown.

"My goodness gracious. Who's the adult in your family?" Grandma's head shook while the coffee grinder whirred. "Honest to Pete, I don't know what gets into your mother sometimes."

Jenna giggled, but just a short giggle. She clapped a hand over her mouth. "Sorry, Grandma, I'm not laughing at you, I just like 'Honest to Pete.'" Jenna felt a frown taking over her face muscles. "I hope it's okay. I collect things people say, like Grandpa says, 'Who'd a thunk it,' and 'Don't get me going.'"

The aroma of fresh ground coffee filled the kitchen. Grandma left it in the grinder and gathered Jenna up in her pink bathrobe arms and hugged. Zeke was busy making noises like some cartoon character. "Zap, zing, zonk, pschew."

"Jenna, my dear heart, you are a grandmother's delight.

Sometimes I truly do wonder who's more the adult, you or your mom." She kissed Jenna's cheek and leaned back and smiled.

Jenna smiled, too, but she answered from thoughts she'd run through her head since last night. "Both of us, I guess. Mom says that's what happens when a woman becomes a single parent, which Mom is in a way because Dad's never with us. Mom has to earn all the money, and I have to help out at home."

Grandma's eyes got dewy, and she patted Jenna's back, just patted and patted and blinked and blinked. "Well, your grandfather and I want to make things easier for all of you. That's why you're living here. And you shouldn't have to help out so much. You should be spending time with your friends."

Jenna looked away from her grandma's eyes. "I don't exactly have any friends."

"That will change once you've been here a bit longer. Pretty girl like you and so smart."

"Smart isn't exactly important."

"It most certainly is. Smart gets you through a whole lot of things life sends your way. Keeps you out of trouble pretty can get you into."

"I hope it helps get me through today with Mom. She's not going to let it drop about me jumping in after that little girl. She'll keep saying that was the dumbest thing I ever did."

Grandma nodded and smiled and hugged Jenna again.

"You know your mom, all right, but this time you've got Grandpa and me on your side."

"Vrrrooom." Zeke crashed into their legs, slithered up, and pasted his skinny body to them. "Me, too, Jenna, I'm on your side."

"Oh, Zeke," Grandma said and hugged him, too.

They were all in a huddle when Grandpa came into the kitchen. "Sure is a noisy place for a Sunday morning." He went straight outside for the Sunday paper, brought it to the kitchen table, and pulled out the local section. His eyes scanned its front page.

Jenna looked at him and then at Grandma, but neither met her eyes. Grandpa always started with sports. Grandma said he read the print right off the pages and told her more than she ever wanted to know about the Mariners and Seahawks and Sonics. Those were all Seattle teams. Tacoma, where they lived, didn't exactly have any major league teams. Grandpa followed high school sports, too, but there wasn't much to follow at the end of June.

Jenna watched her grandpa's eyes. They moved over and down the front page of the local section. He shook his head without looking up and opened the paper. His eyes moved some more, then stopped. He held the paper up in both hands and shook it until it was inside out. He folded it down and then across. Grandma left the coffee dripping and went to stand behind Grandpa. Whatever Grandpa found to read wasn't good news. Jenna wondered where kids her age went when they ran away.

Then Grandma said, "Well, now, that's not so bad," and dusted off her hands.

Grandpa brushed the paper with the back of his hand. "Not so bad until somebody gets hold of it and starts asking questions."

"There're no names…"

"Not in the paper there're not, but names got written down all over the place. Soon as some busybody that wants to know sees this and starts snooping, there'll be names. You can mark my bet."

Mark my bet. Jenna needed to add that to her journal. "What…what does it say?"

Grandpa cleared his throat. Then he cleared it again. "Says a child tripped and fell into the chilly waters of Puget Sound from the McNeil Island float Saturday afternoon. A second child jumped in after the first in a good Samaritan attempt at rescue. A corrections officer brought both to the surface within seconds. Department of Corrections personnel, including hospital staff, tended to both children, who were transported to Steilacoom on the regular ferry run. Both were treated at a local hospital and released."

Jenna let out the breath she'd been holding. "That means the little girl is okay, right?"

Her grandma smiled, but her eyes were kind of teary, and she pulled Jenna in for another hug. "It means just exactly that. You don't have to worry about that little girl one more minute, Jenna."

"Now alls Jenna gots to worry about is Mom."

"All Jenna has to worry about, Zeke," Jenna said.

"'Specially if Mom tied one on, huh Jenna?"

"Zeke MacDonald, where do you get such talk?" Grandma Randall released Jenna and looked at Zeke.

"From my dad. He told me about tying one on, and he don't mean with no rope, neither."

Grandma Randall looked at Zeke and then at Grandpa. "I tell you."

Jenna backed away all the way to the basement door, which led down to her room. She wasn't exactly running away; she was just taking a time out. Grandpa dug through the paper until he found the sports section. Jenna heard him say, "Don't get me going," as she closed the door.

Chapter Seven

Jenna heard feet on the basement stairs, then a knock on her door and Zeke whispering her name.

"You can come in, Zeke."

"Jenna, you can come outside and play with me if you want. Cuz I have to be quiet a little longer. Grandma said."

Jenna had been so far off in her journal mind that she'd forgotten Zeke. He didn't have friends here, either. He didn't have a pool to jump into or trees to climb.

"I don't feel much like playing, but we could draw. We could sit under Grandma's flowering plum tree in the backyard and draw birds like Dad does. Or Grandma's tree."

When they first moved in, their grandma said, "You should have been here just a little sooner. You'd have seen my Blireiana in all her glory. Rosy pink blossoms on every branch and twig." Jenna thought it was a name her grandma made up until Grandma explained it was genus and species. Prunus blireiana. Jenna looked it up, which was a challenge because of the spelling. She didn't mind the challenge. It was something to do.

"You mean the Beery Anna tree, huh?" Zeke said, a sparkle in his eye. That's what he'd thought their grandma said. Then the sparkle left, and he turned serious. "Sometimes I draw good, huh Jenna?"

"You draw quite well, Zeke. Here, help me carry some things. I'll get the quilt Grandma lets us use outside." Jenna gave Zeke a box with odd pieces of paper and assorted colored pencils. She grabbed her journal with the new picture of her dad and her taped in and stationery to write him a letter. Grandma had put the other picture on the front of the refrigerator.

Grandma's tree had reddish-purple leaves and big roots that stuck up in the lawn. Grandpa said it made that corner of the yard a real mess with moss in the grass from all the shade, and he ought to cut it down. Grandma just rolled her eyes and said the tree had been there when they moved in and would likely be there when they moved out.

Jenna spread the quilt and sat. Zeke plopped on his stomach with a stack of paper. "I can start at the bottom, huh? To draw the tree? Cuz it's a drawing, so the rule about starting at the top don't count."

"Doesn't count," Jenna said. "Starting at the bottom's fine. You can sketch the roots and then the trunk and then branches and leaves."

While Zeke sketched, Jenna started a page in her

journal. She wrote, The Dumbest Thing I Ever Did at the top. If it turned out okay, she'd copy it as a letter to her dad.

Yesterday I did something that really, really upset Mom. The dumbest thing ever. I jumped off the float to rescue a little girl who fell in. There were any number of people who could have handled the situation, but I squirted past them. I think Mom's worried that the whole world will find out, and she'll get kicked out of her paralegal program. The program wants students with clean records. That means they don't want criminals, which Mom isn't. It's just that sometimes she gets treated like one.

Zeke stuck his paper between Jenna and her journal page. "Jenna? How's this?"

He'd drawn tree roots with one running off the page and one with a knotty bump. He'd shaded the tree trunk and branches and drawn dangling leaves.

"That's very good, Zeke. I do believe you have Dad's talent." She smiled at him, and then frowned at his puzzled look.

"Does that mean I'll go to prison when I grow up?"

"No. Absolutely not. Dad didn't go to prison for drawing well."

"I know. He went for…" Zeke's arms and hands formed an invisible gun with a finger on the trigger. "…for you know what." He tipped his head and squinted his eyes. "Jenna, are you a damn Indian? Just like Dad?"

Jenna's shoulders dropped, and she sagged forward. Their mom called her that sometimes, which worried her.

While Zeke sketched, Jenna started a page in her journal.

The *damn Indian* part and the *just like her dad* part. She wasn't quite sure what made an Indian different from any other person. Or how she was just like her dad. They both liked to read; that must be what her mom meant, because Jenna didn't like to kill things, not even spiders. Not that Bernie MacDonald wanted to kill that man. But he had been out hunting with a rifle that day, which meant he intended to kill something.

"Indians are just people like anyone else, Zeke. Sometimes Mom says things she doesn't really mean."

Zeke tipped his head left, then right. "Mean's a funny word, huh? Sometimes it stands for *not nice* and sometimes it stands for *I mean it, Zeke. You sit down and shut up right now.*"

He sounded so much like their mom that laughter squirted out of Jenna's throat. Zeke laughed, too. They were both on their backs laughing when their grandma came out onto the back porch.

"Jenna, there's a phone call for you."

That stopped her laugh and sent her heart pounding clear up into her ears. Who would call her? Her dad would call her mom; her best friend Crystal, from Monroe, had a long-distance block on the phone. It must be about yesterday. Jumping in the water after that little girl. The dumbest thing she'd ever done. She closed her journal and took it with her to the house.

"Who?" she mouthed before she picked up the receiver from the kitchen counter.

Grandma Randall shook her head, but she didn't look

really worried like she would if it was someone from the prison.

"Hello?" Jenna said.

"Hi, how's it going? What's happening? Do you know who this is?"

Before Jenna could answer, the caller said, "It's Sara. Like, from school. So, how's it going?"

"Fine." Jenna looked at the yellow and white kitchen where she'd cooked Zeke's breakfast and wondered why it all looked so unfamiliar.

"So, what did you decide about your birthday? Next weekend? Remember, we like asked you the last day of school? Are you inviting us all roller-skating? That's what we like to do on birthdays."

"Oh." Ms. Zalinsky, their homeroom teacher, had announced summer birthdays just before school ended. On the last day of school, the Snoops' four leaders asked Jenna what she planned for her birthday. She'd said she might be visiting her dad.

"Your real dad or your pretend dad?" Dori, the Asian Snoop, asked. She lived with her mom and stepdad and visited her real dad for two weeks during the summer.

"Skate where?" Jenna said into the phone. She had skated at the trailer park, but her skates were too small now.

"At the *skating* rink. Sorta just down the hill. Only it's too far to walk, so your mom picks us up and takes us there and brings us home after and stays in the party room during. Unless she skates, like Lori's mom."

"Um, I'm not sure…"

"We'll help you plan it. Lori and me, we'll come over to your place after while and talk about it, okay?"

"Um, Sara? My mom's not feeling well today. It might not be a good idea for you to come here." Her mom wasn't even up yet, but Jenna knew what to expect on Sundays after Saturday visits to the prison. And today would be worse than usual.

"Nonsense," Grandma Randall said from right behind Jenna.

"We can, like, stay outside. Or in your room, we'll be quiet. We want to see your room. And stuff."

What stuff? Jenna wondered while Sara talked to her phone ear and Grandma talked to her kitchen ear. Jenna's head kind of ached, and then Sara said, "See ya, it'll be fun, bye," and Jenna looked at the silent phone.

"You see, dear, you do have friends. I told you that would change soon enough." Grandma had a nice smile, one that made her eyes shine and drew little lines on her soft cheeks. Grandma tried so hard to make everything right for them, but it was a little like an egg dropped on the floor. You really can't put it back together again.

"Sara's not exactly my friend. She's just this girl who knows my birthday is next weekend. She wants me to have a party."

"Well, I'd say we can arrange that easily enough, Jenna."

"I don't think so, Grandma. I don't think it's going to be easy at all. Sara said something about roller-skating. At a roller rink. Sort of down the hill, but I don't know what hill she means." Jenna wished her grandma didn't look quite so pleased. "And the mom has to drive all the kids."

Grandma's hands came together like applause for something she really liked. "Why, I imagine we can sort that out. Your grandfather and I can find our way to the roller rink if your mom's not available. We used to roller skate when I was a girl. They played music, and oh my, it felt like we floated around that floor."

"I don't think my mom would really go for all that. It would take money, which she doesn't have." Jenna rolled her lips in between her teeth and bit a little to remind her eyes not to get all watery.

"You leave your mom and the money to me. You just get busy making friends."

"And Sara said they're coming over later to help me plan without waiting to be invited. They already know where I live. And they want to see my room."

"Good, it's about time you have friends over, and your room is yours to show."

"What…what am I supposed to say when they ask questions? Like, '*Why do you live with your grandparents?*' And '*What does your dad do?*'"

One of Grandma's hands flew up to her lips and rested there for a few seconds. "Well, how about this? You live here so your mom can go back to school, and your dad's responsibilities have him away just now. Do you think that will work?"

Jenna nodded. "It might." The part about her mom

would work, because it was true. But the part about her dad was going to trip her. She just knew it would. Sometimes she wished she could just tell and get it over with. Just say, My dad's in prison. He killed a man, but he had to or he'd be the one dead.

She wouldn't tell, though. That would upset her mom. Living with an unhappy mom was hard. Maybe even harder than having a dad in prison. And telling would be the end of any hope of joining the Snoops.

Chapter Eight

Jenna put her journal away between the mattress and springs of her bed, where she kept two others already filled. Then she worried someone would sit on the end of the bed and bend them, so she moved them into a dresser drawer with her underwear and socks. Some girls could be snoopy, but she was pretty sure no one would look through her underwear drawer. She just didn't know what *stuff* Sara meant when she said, "*See your room and stuff.*"

Jenna had her familiar things in the room: bed and dresser, desk and boom box (a small one, barely big enough to be called that), bookcase and books. She also had a rocking chair her grandma slipcovered, and throw rugs on the floor.

"That floor is too cold for bare feet," Grandma had said when Jenna first moved in.

"Floor's glued down on cement. What do you expect?" Grandpa said.

"That's not a criticism," Grandma said. "The floor is perfectly nice, it's just cold."

It was all nice—done in pale greens, Jenna's favorite. She taped her dad's animal and bird sketches around the room. Grandma said that gave the room a personal touch. So did the evergreen-tree print curtains Grandma made for the window, which was up by the ceiling. When the curtains were open, Jenna looked out at the bottom of shrubs. If anyone walked by she saw feet and legs. And one time Sara and Lori when they bent down to snoop.

The only bad thing about her room was getting to it. She had to cross the basement, which had Grandma's laundry area in one corner, and Grandpa's tools and work-benches everywhere else. It dawned on Jenna that her basement bedroom wasn't the best place to be when Sara and Lori arrived. And she didn't know what to wear. She bit a piece of loose skin off one finger, then searched her other fingers for another to bite. She hadn't done any serious hangnail biting for months.

Jenna grabbed a book and went upstairs. Her mom was up, finally, holding her head, sipping coffee, and reading the story in the paper.

"Good Samaritan." It didn't sound like a good thing at all, the way Jenna's mom said it. "You'd better hope names never come out. Do you hear me, young lady? Because if names come out, and I get kicked out of the paralegal program, you're going to pay."

"Pay how?" Jenna asked.

Grandma put an arm around Jenna's shoulder. "Now

now, Lynn, that's enough. I can't imagine a program that operates like that. How about some French toast with that coffee?'"

"What do you know about how programs operate, Mom? The director said at orientation, 'No one with criminal records.'"

"Far as I know, you've got no record, Lynnie," Grandpa said. "Might be you should give up your Saturday nights out if you want to keep it that way."

"That's enough," Grandma said. "Jenna has friends coming, and about time. Now, close that newspaper. I'm going to clean this kitchen before those girls get here."

Jenna tiptoed away, across the living room to the front porch. She had read a chapter when Lori and Sara showed up. Lori had smoothed the kinks out of her hair and flipped up the ends. Some ends had purple tips. Sara had her brown hair pulled back and held with a silver clip. Stray hair poked out here and there. Sara worked to get the strays right. They both wore shorts and T-shirts and sandals. So did Jenna. She'd done that much right.

Everyone was polite through introductions. Grandma offered juice and cookies, but Lori said they'd wait; they wanted to see Jenna's room first. Grandpa opened the basement door and waved them down. Laundry detergent and sawdust and machine oil smells mixed together in the stairwell air. Jenna led the way. Her heart pounded so loud she could barely hear when Grandpa called out, "You watch your step, now."

"This is way cool, a room off by itself," Lori said.

Sara moved through the room, her eyes taking it all in. "Can you, like, play your music however loud you want?"

"Not exactly. My grandpa has a workshop down here, which is what all the stuff is about. And sound carries up, anyway."

Lori sat in the slipcovered chair and hitched one long leg over its arm. Her skin was golden brown, not reddish like C/O Hooper's, the woman officer on the boat from McNeil Island. Jenna thought about that for a minute. The little girl's skin was different, too. Not reddish and not golden; just brown. Jenna was so busy thinking about skin-tone that she sort of jumped when Lori said, "How come you live with your grandparents?"

"Mostly so my mom can go back to school. It's a career move." She was worried what the next question might be so she added, "My dad's away right now. My grandma says it makes good economic sense, you know, to live in one house."

"So, are you going to have a skating party for your birthday?" Sara was fiddling with her hair and the clip and watching the mirror while she talked. She pulled some hair loose. A dad being away wasn't of interest to her. Maybe it didn't interest Lori, either. Maybe dads just plain didn't matter to the Snoops.

"I haven't exactly asked my mom yet." Jenna saw Lori's eyes narrow, and her head move forward a bit. "But my grandma said it should be okay. We just need to know how it works. The parent-giving-rides part. See, my mom works odd shifts. And she has to study." On an outward breath she added, "And who to invite."

Lori unhitched her leg. "Okay, here's how it works. There's our group, which is the Howard's Girls, only we don't go by that name since…whenever. Rule number one: you always invite the four who started the group, which is me and Sara and Dori and Kara."

Sara moved her eyes from the mirror to Lori. "Us and two more might be enough, since we're, like, evaluating her for the group."

Sara moved her eyes to Jenna. So did Lori. Jenna's insides jumped like when she was little and her mom drove fast down and up the butterfly dip in a road they took from the trailer park to town. They were evaluating her for the group. She didn't like being evaluated, but she wanted to be part of their group. She wanted friends. One friend would be nice. She saw Sara putting the question together before the words came out.

"So, what are you? Like, I'm Irish American, and Lori is African American. Big duh, like that's hard to figure out. And Dori is Asian American, which in her case is Korean, and Kara's mother came from Australia and has this really neat accent."

Jenna looked at one and then the other and then the high window. She should have opened it so some air could get in.

"Like, we thought you might be Mexican American, which we don't have one of those, but you said no, you're not. But you're not exactly just white, like me."

"She means Caucasian," Lori said. "Borrrrinnng."

"I'm three-eighths Native American Indian." Jenna gulped in a breath. "And the rest boring, I guess." She tried to laugh, but it didn't exactly work. "Grandpa and Grandma Randall, and my mom, are like, English, Scot, German, and who knows." Like? Did that come out of her mouth?

"Indian? Like, from a reservation?" Sara exaggerated her eyes open, and moved her head toward Jenna.

"Not exactly. From Canada. My dad is a Canadian Indian. Three-fourths Indian and one-fourth French Canadian. He thinks. He was adopted, so he's not exactly sure." Now her stomach had frogs in it leaping toward her throat, and her heartbeat filled her ears, which were hot. Her armpits were upside-down pools, and she needed to run upstairs to the bathroom. She picked at a spot on one finger, but no more skin wanted to come loose.

Sara looked at Lori. "That might, like, work. Huh, Lori?"

"Depends." Lori pushed her lips forward and scrunched one eye. "On what you're into. Like sports or music or art."

"Or boys." Sara giggled.

"See, Sara's really into this boy, Michael Perez, which is why she hoped you were Mexican American. Me, I'm into basketball. I'm the center. When we get to high school, I'll probably be center there my first year. I've got brothers, and I don't need no boyfriend telling me what I already know. Are you into basketball?" Lori's squinted eyes studied Jenna.

"Um, not really. I used to play soccer. Before we moved."

"Soccer? That means we should invite Andi. She's really into soccer. I'm into art, too, I like to draw." Lori looked at the pictures Jenna had on the walls. "Faces, mostly. People faces, but these animals and birds are good, did you draw them?"

"My dad. He's into wildlife." Without any finger skin to bite, Jenna nibbled on a spot inside her mouth.

"Lori, if we invite Andi, that's seven. We, like, have to invite Mari and Rika. And there's me and you and Dori and Kara. And with the birthday girl. That makes eight; that's an even number." Sara said that while she looked at the pictures, but they didn't seem to interest her the same way they interested Lori. "Lori likes even numbers. So, is your dad, like, in Canada right now?"

"No, not right now. He's from there. From Vancouver Island, which is hard to get to because of ferry schedules." Jenna bit her lips together. There her mouth went, running on ahead of her.

"I remember on the last day of school you said you might, like, visit your dad. Like, go with your grandparents," Sara said. "Lori says I can't keep a thought in my head, except MP, which is Michael Perez, but she's wrong. I kept that."

"Big hooray!" Lori did something with her hands and her hair, some gesture that Jenna didn't exactly get. "Well, we gotta go. I have to watch my little brothers. We'll call later with phone numbers."

"Phone numbers?" The spot inside Jenna's mouth tasted coppery.

"So you can call about your skating party," Sara said. "Duh, girl."

"Oh, yeah." Jenna went back in her mind to the part about who to invite. The four who started the group, plus two more, plus Andi, plus herself was way more than her mom could fit in the car. "About my mom driving…"

"It's never a problem," Lori said. "My mom always helps. She has a van and she likes to skate."

They trooped up the stairs, Jenna first, and into the kitchen. Sara's eyes went straight to the refrigerator to the Polaroid picture Jenna's grandma put there. Sara's legs followed where her eyes went. Jenna's legs turned to Jell-O.

"Is this your dad? Because he looks way cool, like MP. Where was it taken?"

The island where he lives was what Jenna meant to say, but no words came out of her open mouth. Oh, why had Grandma put that stupid picture on the refrigerator? Then her grandma was there. "Are you girls ready for your cookies now? And a soft drink?"

Sara looked at Lori, who said, "Sure."

Jenna closed her mouth. No words meant no lies.

Next thing, they were out on the porch, sitting on Grandma Randall's nice white wicker chairs with the blue print cushions. Grandma brought cookies and juice on a tray, and set it on the white wicker table. Zeke rode up on his bike. All the way up, right onto the porch, which was against the rules. Grandma said, "Zeke," and Lori said, "Little brothers are the worst." Grandma brought more cookies, and Grandpa came out. He meant to be friendly,

Jenna knew, but it didn't exactly work. Lori and Sara drank their drinks and took two cookies each and left.

"We'll call, girl," Lori said.

Jenna sank into a porch chair and found the breath she'd lost in the kitchen. Her chest ached like her heart had the flu. "Ohhh," she said, that was all. Sara's question was still hanging there, in the air, not the whole question, just the part about where the picture was taken.

Chapter Nine

Jenna needed to run off the tension that came from avoiding lies, which popped up from avoiding truths. She changed into her old running shoes, the ones that were a bit small, and called out, "I'm headed for the park." Grandpa said Howard Park seemed a safe enough place during daylight hours, and the paths made for a good run; he could see that. But no hanging around Howard Middle School. Vandals had hit the place more than once.

Jenna's mom caught her by the wrist. "I'm not through with you, Jenna. Having friends drop in is not going to make me forget. You're just lucky I have to get to work. At a job I hate, by the way." She dropped Jenna's arm and went out the door.

Jenna rubbed her wrist. Her mom's shifts changed all the time, which caused no end of problems for Grandma, who planned the meals. Jenna was used to her mom's changing schedule. She and Zeke ate canned soup and sandwiches for dinner when they lived in the trailer park.

Grandma said that wouldn't do. They needed real meals with fresh fruits and vegetables, which she served with speeches about why they were good for you. Jenna wished her mom could be more like her grandma.

At the park Jenna wove her way around boys on skateboards and scooters and moms pushing strollers. Sometimes a dad pushed a stroller, but mostly dads without moms played with older kids. Maybe the mom was home vacuuming and cooking. Or maybe the parents were divorced, and the dad was having his weekend with the children. She thought about the Snoops, who were evaluating her, and got turned around and left the park at the wrong entrance. That happened sometimes. Her mind got busy with worries, and she got turned around. She ran two blocks before she realized it was the wrong direction.

When she got home, Zeke was in trouble for going off on his bike without telling where he was going. He was in time-out on a chair in the kitchen with his hands folded in his lap. Grandma was browning a pot roast. The kitchen smelled like garlic. It usually smelled like fried onions and sometimes like homemade cookies. Grandpa was in the living room watching baseball on television.

"I was looking for you, Jenna. Grandma said you went to the park, and I wanted to ask you something."

Jenna looked at their grandma, who nodded. "It's okay. Zeke may talk."

"What, Zeke? What did you want to ask me?"

"I wanted to ask could I come with you? Cuz you're my onliest friend since school got out."

"Only," Jenna said. "What are the rules about riding your bike?" She corrected him and asked him to repeat the rules from old habit. Her mind was still busy with the Snoops and being in trouble with her mom and what it would be like to have a dad.

Zeke tipped his head one way and then the other. His eyes sparkled. "No riding in the big streets. Stay out of Graham's driveway. Move to the right when cars come in the park."

Jenna counted to ten in her head. "Those are trailer park rules, Zeke. They don't exactly fit here. What are Grandma's and Grandpa's rules?"

"Always tell where you're going, and I did that, I said, 'I'm going with Jenna,' and Grandma said, 'Let Jenna be,' and I said I wanted to ask you something, and Grandma said it could wait. But it couldn't. It's another something; not the could I come with you one."

She knew Zeke was worked up. His little bottom was all over the chair seat. "What something is it?"

"Jenna? Can I come to your birthday party? Grandma says you're going to have a birthday party at a roller skating place. Can I be invited? I hardly never been to a birthday party."

Jenna let Zeke's grammar go and closed her eyes. She hadn't thought about that. Who would watch Zeke while their grandparents and the Snoops were at the roller rink? Maybe if he had one special friend with him it would work. She didn't know much about birthday parties. She looked at Grandma, who just waited with her eyebrows lifted high. Jenna gave the best answer she could. "I don't know yet. I think it depends."

Zeke's chair rocked. "You sound like Mom. It depends. That means 'No way,' right?"

Grandma turned the meat to brown the other side. She used a big, two-prong fork. The meat sizzled, and steam rose up in front of her face. "When young ladies turn thirteen they need to be with their friends now and then without little brothers. When your birthday comes, we'll plan a special party for you."

"Who's going to see to me, Grandma? Jenna always sees to me. It's a rule, like where I can ride my bike."

Zeke was right. Jenna did see to him. The last few years she'd seen to him more than their mother had. He needed a dad as much as she did. Maybe more. At least she had stories her dad told about when she was born. About how much he loved her and how he played with her and fed her. Zeke didn't have even that.

Grandma set down the fork and went to Zeke and pulled him to her. "We're going to see to you, Zeke. Your grandfather and I will see to you. We're not going to leave you alone—not for one minute, but we need your help. We need you to remember to leave our property only with permission and to be back on time. Will you remember that?"

"Uh huh. Can I be out of time-out?"

"You may."

Zeke shoved the chair back to where it belonged at the table. Grandma smiled. Zeke turned a cartwheel right in the kitchen. Grandma frowned. Jenna's hand flew to cover her smile. Then Grandma laughed.

"Zeke, I need you to save your cartwheels for outside. Inside cartwheels push my heart rate too high."

"Okay, Grandma," Zeke said. "Come on Jenna. You count while I stand on my head."

Jenna followed Zeke into the backyard. Behind her she heard Grandma say to Grandpa, "Honest to Pete, that boy's busier than a tree full of monkeys."

Jenna helped Zeke with his headstands and handstands and cartwheels before dinner and played board games with him after dinner. She was waiting for her dad's Sunday night call. Had he heard about the dumbest thing she'd ever done? Would he think it was a bad thing like her mom thought? She didn't get to find out that night because her mom covered for someone on the next shift, and her grandpa refused the call when it came from her dad.

"Why'd you do that?" Grandma said.

"Because Lynnie's not here," Grandpa said.

"Jenna wanted to talk to him."

"Better let Lynnie talk first is my thinking."

Jenna listened for Grandma's answer to that, but there wasn't one. She finished the game with Zeke and went to her room to read. She stayed awake for a long time, then slept late the next morning. When she opened the door from the basement stairs, her mom and grandma were in the kitchen. Jenna knew they'd been arguing. She could feel it.

"It's in the paper again—the whole thing—good Samaritan and all," Jenna's mom said. "I hope you're happy. I hope I don't have to divorce your dad over this. To keep my place in my program. Then you'd never get to see him. Think about that, Jenna."

Jenna's mom enrolled in the paralegal program at the community college in April. She had one quarter under her belt (Grandpa's words) and she'd gotten all A's.

Jenna's grandma started talking before her mom finished. "Let it be, Lynn, give the child time to wash her face and wake up a little."

Jenna escaped by going to the bathroom. For a minute she thought she would vomit. Divorce her dad? Then what would happen to him? How would she get to see him? Underage kids had to be accompanied by an adult to visit the prison. That was the rule.

"Why?" she whispered when she came out of the bathroom. "Why would they have it in the paper again?"

Grandma patted her arm. "Oh, they do that all the time with Sunday stories. Print them again on Monday. Who knows why? Don't dwell on it, Jenna. You have a party to plan, and your mom has a class to get to." She turned to Jenna's mom, and her voice sounded harsh. "Just go on to your class, Lynn. Your program. Let Jenna be a young girl for once in her life. Let her be excited about a birthday party."

Jenna tried to keep the divorce threat out of her mind, but it was there. Grandma said it was just that—an idle threat. She made the arrangements with the skating rink and ended up talking to the moms when Jenna called about the party. All seven girls already knew about it. Lori and Sara had seen to that. Grandma and Lori's mom had about a hundred phone conversations. Well, five. It turned out Lori's mom would help with the driving and supervision, but she had to take her two youngest boys, which meant Zeke might as well be included. She popped over on her way to the grocery store so the boys could meet.

"I'm Sandra Johnson." Lori's mom held out her hand to Grandma. "This is Rydell. He's eleven, and this one's Terell. He's nine. It's nice to meet you, Mrs. Randall."

Jenna watched her grandma take Mrs. Johnson's hand and pat it. Mrs. Johnson was a major surprise. A white surprise. That made Lori half white. Half boring. In about two seconds Zeke and Terell were out on the front lawn turning somersaults.

"I swear, that one has more energy than the other four combined," Mrs. Johnson said. "Go keep an eye on him, Rydell. I signed both of them up for about every day-camp program Parks and Rec offers. Are you sending Zeke?"

"Why, I hadn't even thought of that, Mrs. Johnson, but it sounds like a good idea. We're trying to help our daughter with the children while she trains for a new career."

"Call me Sandy. If you send Zeke, we could share driving. But first things first. We're here to plan Jenna's party."

"And I'm Jean," Jenna's grandma said. "Jenna's named for me. It's a variation."

Jenna could hardly wait to get to her journal. That was

the first she'd heard of being named for Grandma. Why hadn't she figured it out? She was smart enough. Why hadn't her mom told her? She knew the answer to that one—her mom didn't exactly have time to sit around and chat about things.

"Here's how it generally works, Jean," Sandy Johnson said.

Jenna relaxed. Her grandma and Lori's mom were in charge of the party. She went out to the porch, sat on the top step, and watched Rydell teach Zeke and Terell to walk on their hands. It felt good to sit there and watch and not worry for a minute.

"Look, Jenna, I'm not tipping," Zeke said just as he fell over backward. He scrambled to his feet. "I can show Dad, huh? On our next visit. Huh, Jenna?"

Jenna was on her feet, shushing and giving Zeke a warning look. His head fell forward, but not before she saw the sadness come in his eyes. It wasn't right; it just wasn't.

"You can show Dad after you practice. After you're really good. Someday soon, I promise." Jenna had her eyes focused right on Zeke's now, and they said the rest. *Don't say extended family visit. Don't say visiting room. Don't say prison.*

Chapter Ten

After that, Jenna didn't even try to relax. Relaxing would be for after her first ever real birthday party. She was being evaluated by the Snoops and glared at by her mom and investigated by the Department of Corrections. She was at the center of the McNeil Island Float Incident. That's what the DOC called it. They sent an investigator to the house to talk to all of them, including Zeke. Jenna's mom had to rearrange her work shift, and her grandpa had to miss most of the baseball game on TV. Everyone sat at the kitchen table for the interview. Grandma wanted to make coffee, but the investigator said no thanks; he needed to get right to the questions. He opened his briefcase and got out a stack of papers and a tape recorder.

"Just a minute," Grandpa Randall said, "we're not answering questions with a tape recorder running."

The investigator argued, but Grandpa said no, they'd agreed over the phone to an informal discussion, and that's what it would be. The investigator turned on the recorder and said, "This is Sidney Plunket," and then he said the date and the place and McNeil Island Float Incident and that Mr. Randall refused to permit use of the recorder. He put it back in his briefcase, pulled out a pen and lined tablet and a pair of glasses. He put the glasses on the end of his nose and looked over the top of them at Jenna, and said, "Okay, you first."

Jenna answered the questions and told about the baby losing his shoe on the ramp and how steep it was and how hard for the mom with four children. She told about the shoe being dropped once at the depot when they were boarding the bus and the two girls holding hands while they picked it up.

"Too bad that's not on tape," Sidney Plunket said. "Those are good details." Then he turned to Grandpa, who was closest to Jenna at the time of the incident.

Grandpa answered questions. Grandma hushed Zeke about a hundred times. Jenna's mom scowled and kept her arms crossed. In the end, they all told the same story. Then Sidney Plunket asked the big question.

"Why did you jump in after her, Jenna, when there were officers and other staff on the float?"

"I know why," Zeke said. He stood up like he was making a speech and told about falling into the pool at the trailer park and Jenna jumping in to save him. Lots of times. "I broke the rule, but Jenna never told, so it's not our mom's fault cuz she didn't know, she's doing the best she can with us. The end." He sat down without rocking his chair.

This is what Jenna's journal mind saw: Grandma

smiled; Grandpa coughed into his hand, but he smiled, too; Lynn closed her eyes and lowered her head, but a tear ran out and sat on her cheek until she wiped it away. Sidney Plunket's pen flew across the paper. He wrote for a long time. At least five minutes. When he was through, he took off his glasses and looked at Lynn. He squinted his eyes like he really needed to keep his glasses on.

"Mrs. MacDonald, I need to remind you that it is your responsibility to see that your children obey DOC visiting rules, or you will all lose your visiting privileges."

"Yes, I know," Lynn said, and Jenna could tell it was one of those times when the wife, who didn't do anything wrong, was getting treated like a criminal, too. It wasn't fair to her mom.

Sidney Plunket put his tablet back in the briefcase and pulled out some forms, which he read aloud. They said all concerned agreed the float incident was resolved, and the Department of Corrections was not responsible and could not be sued.

Grandpa said, "So, now we're getting to the crux of the matter."

Zeke said, "Crutch," and limped around like he was leaning on one.

"Crux, Zeke." Grandma reined him in and held him. "Like heart. Or center."

Lynn said, "Daddy, just sign so we can be through with this."

They signed. Sidney Plunket stood up and clutched his brief case and scrunched his eyes at Jenna. "All in all, that was a pretty brave thing you did. I'd be proud if my daughter went to someone's rescue."

Jenna tried to smile, but somehow tears were in her eyes. She tried to swallow so she could say, thanks, but something stuck in her throat.

"We are proud," Grandpa said. "Proud, and more than a little concerned about how you folks handle visitors. You might want to think about that."

"Daddy!" Lynn said.

"Lynn, you let your father speak his mind," Grandma said.

"Mr. Randall has a point," Sidney Plunket said. "Off the record, I'd say such an occurrence anywhere else would earn an award. You folks take care." He went out the door and across the porch and down the steps.

Jenna stayed a bundle of nerves (Grandma's words) the rest of the week. She chewed on her thumb until it bled. Grandma said she should relax. It was just a skating party. She'd skate better if she just relaxed. Jenna didn't say anything, but there was a whole lot more than a skating party in her nerve bundle. Her mom got into a fight with her dad during their Wednesday night phone call and hung up before Jenna got to talk. Did that mean a divorce would be next? Grandpa was operating on his short fuse because someone fiddled with the TV, and he couldn't find the baseball game. He'd already missed most of one that week. Zeke forgot the rules and turned a cartwheel right into the coffee table and sent a vase of flowers and water flying. And a big box with Jenna's gift from her dad arrived insured, which meant Grandma had to sign for it. Besides being insured, it had the fact of being mailed by an inmate stamped top and bottom and all four sides.

Jenna's grandma and mom got into a major discussion about the box.

Grandma said, "Whatever it is, it needs to come out so the box can be burned."

Jenna's mom said, "It might not be wrapped inside. They usually aren't allowed to wrap things."

Jenna couldn't stand it anymore and went down to her room to write in her journal. When she came back up, there were big black curls in the fireplace and an odor that went up her nose and then down into her throat. Her grandma was frowning and washing the fireplace glass doors.

"Honest to Pete, cardboard doesn't burn down very well these days. It must be full of glue." She gave the doors another swipe with crumpled newspaper and then she gave Jenna a hug. "You'll like what's inside. I can guarantee that." The frown was gone, replaced with a Grandma smile.

On Saturday morning, Grandma served pancakes with a candle in Jenna's. "You're officially thirteen now; a young lady." She gave Jenna four young adult novels, each wrapped separately because even young ladies like to open gifts. Grandma and Grandpa together gave her shorts and T-shirts for summer and new sandals.

Jenna's mom gave her a box filled with bath and after-bath care items. "For pampering yourself. I want you to know I am proud of you, but I'm worried, too." She gave Jenna a kiss on her forehead. "Let's leave it at that."

Jenna was pretty sure Grandma or Grandpa had warned her to let it go for a while. She'd heard them say that more than once.

Zeke gave her a small box that he shook so she could hear it rattle. Inside were four shiny quarters—the new ones with four different states named on them. "That's one dollar, Jenna. I saved them from my allowance. You shouldn't spend them cuz they're special."

"I promise I won't ever spend them. I'll keep them in this box for ever and ever." Sometimes Zeke did things that made her want to cry.

"'Sides, a dollar's not worth much, Grandpa said so."

Grandma said, "That dollar is worth a whole lot, Zeke, because you saved it yourself," which got Zeke rocking in his chair.

Then it was time for Jenna's gift from her dad. Her mom had found a different box for it, wrapped it, and tucked the card under the bow. The card said he loved her and made the gift for her with love. He'd made the card, a drawing of a forest with animals and birds blended in so it required patience to find them. Jenna opened the package and pushed aside the tissue paper her mom had put in and took in a deep breath.

"It's all hand crafted, Jenna." Her mom's eyes were wet but not runny wet. Jenna thought she sounded proud.

Maybe that meant she wasn't really thinking about divorce.

Jenna looked from her mom to the gift, a wooden box with her favorite hummingbirds carved in the top. They hovered over blossoms. Jenna ran her fingers over the fine carved lines. She liked how hummingbirds could hover, and then back up if they needed to get away. She lifted the box out of the wrapping and set it on the table. It had a bronze lock on the front and a key taped to a note inside.

This box is for your journal and other treasures. When I come home, I will build you a trunk so you can keep journals for all the years to come.

"The man's an artist. Nothing can change that fact," her grandpa said.

It was the nicest thing Jenna had ever heard her grandpa say about her dad. She had to excuse herself to blow her nose. She was a young lady now, which meant she couldn't cry even if she was a bundle of nerves and her dad's present had to be sent from prison.

Chapter Eleven

The skating rink, with its music booming and disco ball reflecting colored lights and seven Snoops talking, was more than Jenna's nerve bundle could handle.

"Where's the restroom?"

Lori's mom pointed her in the right direction. Jenna didn't really need to go. It just gave her more time to worry. *What if* she couldn't skate at all? *What if*... well, she had a million *What If*'s flitting around in her head. She needed to concentrate on something else. Like the rink itself, which reminded her of a cave, though she didn't exactly remember ever being in a cave. She knew things like caves and canyons and ocean beaches from pictures and reading.

The skating rink cave had rails around three sides and rails plus openings for skaters on one side. The colored lights made her dizzy. Or maybe the *What if*s made her dizzy, because she either held her breath or gulped in air.

The music made her feet want to move, and she hadn't even gotten them into skates yet.

Zeke and Terell stumbled around the rink's perimeter, arms wind milling, bumping each other, tumbling, laughing. That would be nice, Jenna thought, to just stagger and laugh and not worry. She concentrated on getting her skates laced the right way. There was probably only one way to lace and tie skates, but she watched the Snoops just in case.

While Jenna worried, Lori, the African American who turned out to be half white, lined them up by skin color. "Me first, then Andi, then Jenna after Andi, then Dori, then Sara, then…"

Jenna lost track after that because Andi started talking to her. Lori was still ordering the others where to sit, and they were giggling and changing places with one skate on and one in their hands. A girl named Rika sat at the far end.

Andi loosened laces in the size ten skates she rented. "Rika's from Iceland, her skin's really white, and her eyes are so pale they look like a window. I'm Pacific Islander. Samoan and Hawaiian, mostly. What are you, Jenna?"

Jenna looked at Andi. She was bigger than Lori's mom, but something about her smile helped Jenna relax. "Native American and French Canadian from my dad, a mixture from my mom."

Lori, whose skates were already laced and tied, was on her feet. "No, no, no, don't tell, I'm going to announce it. Okay everybody. Listen up. Jenna's Indian from her dad and boring from her mom. Don't tell my mom I said that. Catch this, Jenna. Andi wants to play football, and she's bigger than most of the guys, but the school won't let her."

Andi shrugged. "So for now I play soccer."

"I used to play soccer." Jenna concentrated on her own laces, still uncertain where to let her eyes rest. "Until we moved."

"Right on, girl, what position?"

Jenna looked at Andi. "Left half. I'm right handed, but kind of left footed, for some reason."

"Are you for real? I'm left fullback. You can guess why."

Jenna grinned. "It would be hard for right wings to get around you."

"You've got it. Plus I'm slow, so I can't sweep. I stay back where I belong, and when the ball needs to be cleared, I can punch it like hell." Andi looked at Jenna's grandma and Lori's mom, who'd just come into the skate room. "Oops, sorry, I know better. My mouth just runs off on its own sometimes."

"That's what my mom says about me. Words squirt out sometimes, like my brain is taking a nap."

"Give me five," Andi said, and stuck out a broad hand with short, thick fingers. She scrunched her eyes and tipped her head. "Our soccer team could use a left half."

Jenna put her hand up to meet Andi's. It felt good to give five with her.

Lori rolled past them saying, "Quiet, everybody be

quiet. Now here's how it works. We go out in the order we're lined up."

Andi pulled Jenna to her feet. "There's a soccer camp week after next, except it starts Saturday because the Fourth of July is Monday. It's Howard Park. You should come."

"Shut up and grab hands," Lori said and took hold of Andi's.

Andi took Jenna's and whispered, "I've got the information. I'll get your phone number and call you. Let's go."

Everyone was talking and laughing. Maybe they had been all along. Jenna wasn't sure. She'd meant to be last onto the floor, but she was being pulled by Andi and pushed by Dori and the others behind her. "Birthday girl, birthday girl." They skated around the rink like a train on uneven tracks. Jenna's arms beat at the air when they let go. She got her balance but stayed close to the rails. Lori's mom skated onto the floor in hot pink and black spandex. She had a good figure, like Jenna's mom. She went around the perimeter once, then looped and went around again, backward. One by one she grabbed girls hands and took them with her. Mrs. Johnson knew how to skate.

Andi yelled something to Jenna as she skated by. Something about a turn. Next thing, Mrs. Johnson had Jenna's hands.

"Let your legs relax, Jenna. Let them feel the music. I saw you earlier; your head was swaying while you were lacing your skates. Find your balance and then push and glide. Push...glide...there, you've got it."

And just like that, Mrs. Johnson skated off and caught up with Zeke and Terell. Jenna thought she must be some kind of goddess because she got Zeke balanced. By the next song, he looked like a kid who knew how to skate. Not that he kept to that. He and Terell had to be reminded two times to go the right way around the floor and two times to skate, not run.

Andi skated with Jenna on the first call for pairs. Jenna liked that. She didn't once think about biting a hangnail with Andi like she did with Lori and Sara. Then the deejay called, "Trios. Three together now. Threes only; all others off the floor."

Lori and Sara pulled Rika away from Mari; Dori and Kara caught Mari's hand. "Damn," Andi said, "your and Lori's brothers got Mrs. Johnson. Excuse my mouth."

They were almost to the waiting area benches when a boy skated up. "Hey, Andi, you better introduce me, else I be in trouble with Sara, hittin' on a stranger."

"Hey back, MP. This is Jenna, Jenna this is Michael Perez. How come you're here?"

"Me and Sara's in some kind of trouble with her mom, so I can't go to her house for a week. Come on. We catch up with them, make Sara jealous."

And off they went, Jenna in the middle, Andi and MP pulling. Jenna had to watch her feet so she'd quit staring at MP. He had black hair, straight as her own, with one little clump that fell forward toward his eyes. His eyes were black, but with little bonfires in them. He smelled good, like expensive soap, not cheap cologne. Jenna moved her feet to keep up. They caught up with Lori, Sara, and Rika. Sara was in the middle.

"Hey, Sara, lookit here, I got the new girl, maybe I be her date beings it's her birthday." MP put on speed. So did Andi. Jenna went along for the ride.

"MP, you better watch it," Sara yelled.

"I'm watching Jenna. She's real pretty."

Jenna's face felt hot. She watched her skates.

"Hey, Jenna," MP said, "you part Beaner like me?"

"Huh?" Jenna looked at him again and decided he was as good looking as her dad. Which was what got her mom into trouble—falling in love with looks. Jenna had vowed that would never happen to her. But maybe she could understand, just a little. Not that she'd fallen in love. And not that she'd do anything about it. She couldn't even smile. Her chest hurt where her heart hammered.

"Chicana, maybe? Half Mex?"

"Oh. No." Jenna tried to get her insides to settle enough to talk and skate at the same time. "Part Indian."

"Nah, can't be Indian." MP moved his face close to Jenna's and stole her breath, just like that. "I had one of them in my class. She had a red dot between her eyes. You got no red dot."

Andi leaned across Jenna and gave MP a look. "Native American Indian. Don't be stupid. Are you trying to get in trouble with Sara?"

"Sara's not here right now. I'm just being friendly. 'Til she catches up with me."

They circled the floor three more times before the

music wound down and stopped and Sara caught up. And skated right up to MP, chest to chest, and kissed him. On the lips. Right in the middle of the floor. Which was against the rules. The skating rink's rules. And grandma's rules, Jenna was pretty sure. And Mrs. Johnson's, who skated over and whispered, but not very quietly, "None of that, Sara. You know better." Mrs. Johnson hooked arms with MP and skated him to a bench.

Lori said, "Hoo boy, Sara, my mom's on a tear. She warned you. No boys. Next thing, she'll have my dad here."

"It's not my fault, Lori. I didn't invite him, I just, like, said where we were going."

Jenna watched Sara put on a pout and move her eyes to watch MP and Mrs. Johnson. Sara's pout got real, and she made a snorting noise as Mrs. Johnson and MP skated past them. Lori said, "Hoo boy, we should have hoped for *my* dad."

Jenna's eyes followed where Lori looked. There were three boys in look-at-me-I'm-way-cool poses. Frozen in place. And behind them, just as still but not frozen, a large man in a blue uniform that reminded Jenna of McNeil Island corrections officers. His shoulders were as wide as the door behind him. He put his hands on his belt and hoisted it. One hand moved to a holstered gun attached to the belt. Jenna blinked. The man looked like Arnold Schwarzenegger, only darker.

"That's Andi's dad," Sara said. "He's, like, a city cop or something. He's always checking on her."

A policeman. Jenna's insides did the twist. She hadn't done anything wrong. As far as she knew, no one had done anything, but those boys sure froze in place. They looked like a poster. Her insides settled and left Jenna sad. So far Andi was the only Snoop that didn't make her want to start a new hangnail and chew it clear to the knuckle. She'd even imagined they might be friends. But that wouldn't work. Jenna's mom would freak. It was a Lynn MacDonald rule. Do not trust the police.

"*The police are our friends, Mom. They visited school. They said.*"

"*They're not* our *friends, Jenna, don't ever forget that. Don't ever.*"

Andi skated up fast, grabbed Jenna's arms, and twirled. Her skates tangled with Jenna's and they landed in a heap, Andi on top. Lori tried to back away and tangled with Sara, and they piled on top of Andi. The music stopped. From the bottom of the stack, Jenna saw skaters head for the rails. The three Snoops all giggled, so Jenna laughed, too. That went on for about an hour. Well, a minute, and then Mrs. Johnson was there. And Grandma, who looked worried. And Andi's dad, who would not want his daughter to have a friend whose dad was in prison.

Andi skated with Jenna on the first call for pairs...Jenna didn't once think about biting a hangnail...

Chapter Twelve

Mrs. Johnson said, "Okay, let's get you sorted out here and up on your skates. That's no way to treat the birthday girl."

Sara was the first back on her feet. "I didn't, like, invite MP, Mrs. Johnson. Really."

Lori was next. "Duh, Sara, like we're all that dumb we can't figure it out. And now his Mexi-pep friends are here, and they'll be hitting on the other girls like they always do. You are so uncool."

"Lorraine Renae Johnson!" Mrs. Johnson said while she tugged on Andi. "Jenna, give her a push if your arms aren't squished."

Before Jenna could push, Andi was lifted and settled on her feet. "Hi, Daddy, meet my new friend, Jenna MacDonald. She's the one with the birthday. She played left half before she moved here. I want her to try out with us. Jenna, this is my dad. He's one of our soccer coaches."

In that second Jenna knew she'd never play soccer in Tacoma, not if a police officer coached. She put up an arm to be pulled, but Andi's dad knelt beside her. "Mano Tupou. Before we lift you let's make certain you're okay. What's your name?"

Jenna saw the same kindness in Mr. Tupou's eyes that she'd seen in Andi's. He made her feel safe, but he was a policeman, and she was a prison inmate's daughter. Her squirt-bottle brain shot tears out of her eyes. She tried to sit, but Mr. Tupou's hands were on her shoulders.

"Your name?" He smiled. "And the date?"

"Daddy, she's fine, I didn't break anything, I'm not *that* heavy."

"Jenna MacDonald. June twenty-fifth, 2005. It's my birthday, and George W. Bush is the president." She swiped at her eyes. She wanted him to let her up. Next thing he'd ask where her parents were. Maybe she'd just turn in her skates and leave. She could never be a Snoop, or whatever they were called. Why had she thought for a minute she could? They'd keep asking questions about her dad, and her mom-voice in her head would keep reminding her of the rules.

"Good, you know the drill. Most soccer players do. Let's get you on your feet and get this birthday party going again." Mr. Tupou lifted her, made sure she was steady, and waved to the deejay. "I'm on duty. I just stopped to meet you, Jenna. I like to know Andrea's friends."

Andi, who'd grabbed one of Jenna's hands, now caught

hold of her dad's arm. He walked toward the door. Andi and Jenna rolled along behind. "Daddy, you're supposed to call me Andi."

Mr. Tupou looked at his daughter and grinned. "I will, soon as it snows back home."

Andi gave her dad's arm a little shove. "Great. My dad always says that. We moved here from Honolulu, where it never snows, and he's from Samoa, where it snows even less. Come on, Jenna, let's try skating backward."

Andi's enthusiasm caught Jenna. Well, okay, Jenna thought, for the rest of this night. It's my birthday. I can have a friend for the rest of this night. They stayed close to the rails and practiced.

"Get rolling, turn, keep rolling," Andi said, and Jenna repeated it, and then they said it together and laughed and skated backward two feet and the music stopped, like it was following them.

The music started again, "Happy Birthday," and the deejay asked for everyone to sing to Jenna, who was celebrating her thirteenth birthday. The whole place sang, and then the Snoops skated Jenna to the party room. A birthday party tablecloth covered the table, and balloons floated above a cake decorated with her name and roses and skates. There were pitchers of soft drinks and special paper plates, cups, and napkins at every place. And presents on another table. Terell and Zeke skated to the presents. Mrs. Johnson turned them around and skated them out of the party room.

"Go, you boys go on, both of you. I'll come find you when it's your turn for cake."

They went—just like that.

Jenna felt her mouth open, but no sound came. Her tongue was stuck behind her lower teeth. Just stuck. Mrs. Johnson skated back and settled Jenna in the chair at the end of the table and put a diamond-studded tiara on her head. Well, a fake one, but neat. The Snoops talked and giggled over the pile-up story. They pointed at Jenna, who was on the bottom, and giggled some more. Jenna's grandma served cake. Voices came too fast for Jenna to sort them out.

"I want a big rose."

"I want a corner piece."

"Me, too."

"I want a skate. Give me the piece with the skate. Oh, please, please."

"Did you see those Mexi-pep boys turn to stone when Andi's dad walked in?"

Most of the Snoops giggled. Sara didn't.

"It wasn't funny. Those boys are really, like, nice. Don't call them Mexi-peps; they don't all eat jalapenos."

"Get over it, Sara, just because they follow Michael Perez doesn't mean we have to like them. They aren't all that nice."

Rika, Jenna thought. That was Rika, and she wasn't giggling. Her cold blue eyes stared straight at Sara.

"Like, what do you mean?" Sara picked a rosebud from her frosting and popped it in her mouth.

"Like, they talk nasty, and you know it, Sara, and I'm not skating with them. And the one they call Dario puts his hands where they're not wanted."

Jenna's grandma stopped right in the middle of pouring drinks.

Mrs. Johnson rapped her knuckles on the table. Her eyes moved from girl to girl. Jenna knew that look. She'd seen her mom give the same one plenty of times.

"That's it. When you girls go back out to skate, you will not skate with those boys. Sara, that means you won't skate with Michael. Mrs. Randall and I can't make them leave, but we can see to it they stay away from you girls. And you from them." Mrs. Johnson's eyes settled on Sara. Then they swept over everyone. "Now, does anyone want another scoop of ice cream?" When no one answered, she said, "Going once, going twice."

Andi waved her hand. "I'll have a scoop, Mrs. Johnson."

"Me, too," Rika said, and right away Lori said, "Me three, Mom," and the giggle-shuffle started again. Mrs. Johnson handed the ice cream scoop to Grandma Randall and said she'd go round up Zeke and Terell before it all melted. Jenna's grandma took over, scooping ice cream, pouring drinks, patting shoulders the way she did.

Jenna had a spoonful of ice cream ready and her mouth open, when it came to her that Mrs. Johnson said she was going after Zeke and Terell, but she was really going to talk to Michael Perez and his friends. Jenna just knew it the way she knew odd things without being told. And Mrs. Johnson was gone way longer than it would take to round up those two cake-sniffing boys.

Zeke and Terell stayed almost quiet, their mouths

busy with cake and ice cream, while Jenna opened her gifts. Lori and Sara gave her four picture frames for her dad's drawings. They were made of wood. Lori said they came from Artco Crafts, if she wanted to take them back. Jenna said they were perfect, which they were. For a minute she thought she was going to cry again. She got hair scrunchies and perfume and nail polish and a journal. It had pressed leaves and flowers on the cover.

"You keep a journal, right?" Dori said. "We talked about that once, remember? In homeroom when Zalinsky made us write an essay, and you knew how."

"Yes." Jenna's eyes were going all damp again, and she had to look down at the cake crumbs and melting ice cream on her plate. She'd never had such a nice journal. And Dori remembered that about her.

Andi handed her a small package, an unwrapped box tied with raffia ribbon. "It's not much. I made it. I hope you like it."

"Oh, I do. I mean, I'm sure I will." Jenna untied the ribbon and opened the box. It held a necklace and a bracelet made of shells.

"They're mostly just puka shells plus a few small cowries. We brought them from Hawaii. I strung them for you myself. The short one's an ankle bracelet. I wear one all summer with my sandals."

"I've never had an ankle bracelet." Jenna looked at Andi. She wished they could be friends, just friends, without worrying about their dads or the Snoops. But that wasn't likely. Jenna was thirteen now. She knew better.

Chapter Thirteen

The next day, Jenna's grandma teased her about being in an after-birthday glow, which she guessed she was. She had all her birthday presents on display on the coffee table, where she could look at them and touch them. She wanted to wait a little longer before she used so much as a scrunchy. She wanted to dream a little longer about having Andi as her friend.

Zeke asked if he could touch her things, just touch them, and had one scrunchy on each wrist. When Grandma made the birthday-glow comment, he put all his fingers together with his thumbs, and then fanned them wide as he could. "Glow, glow," he said, and Grandma laughed.

"Zeke, I believe you will be an actor one day. Maybe even a writer. You have such an imagination."

Zeke stopped, his fingers wide apart. "Is that a good thing, Grandma?"

"Well, it can be, Zeke. Like Jenna's serious nature is a good thing. But both need a balance. Jenna could use some of your silly antics now and then, and you could take a page from her sensible side."

"How do I get a page?" Zeke's fingers were still fanned out.

"Why, you watch her and try to behave like she does. You might pick up a book and read or come give me a hand in the kitchen."

"I already know how to make peanut butter and jelly sandwiches. Jenna showed me when we lived in the trailer park." He slipped the scrunchies from his wrists and set them down exactly where he'd found them.

"That's a good start, Zeke. A very good start."

"It is?" Zeke said and he smiled, and his arms came down, and his fingers relaxed.

Right then Jenna knew for certain she was right about something she'd tried to talk about to her mom. Zeke behaved better when he got good attention. Like Grandma gave him. Her mom had said something like, "What do you expect of me, Jenna? I'm doing this all by myself, don't forget." Except she wasn't. Jenna had always helped with Zeke.

"Jenna, I could teach you some noises. Like farts." Zeke squeezed his palms together so they popped.

Jenna heard a chuckle from behind Grandpa's paper. Grandma lifted her eyes to the ceiling and let out a sigh. "I was thinking more in terms of Jenna's idea of fun. She had fun skating last night. I'm not so sure thirteen-year-old girls want to go around making fart noises. They're young ladies, you know."

"Oh," Zeke said. "I know two things, Grandma. Jenna

likes to play soccer, and she likes to swim." He did crawl strokes with his arms, turning his head to the side to blow. "She taught me, only it didn't take yet. I forget and blow in instead of out."

Grandpa put down his paper. "Maybe it's time for swim lessons. At the Y or one of the park pools. I just read about that somewhere in the sports section."

That's when Jenna's mouth opened and let her thoughts run out. "I'd like to go to soccer camp. There's one at Howard Park. Next week. But it might be too expensive."

Grandpa looked at her and nodded. "We'll look into that, Jenna. No reason you can't do both."

"I should have thought ahead and asked for that for my birthday present. Maybe I could return something." Not the books. She liked having her own books.

"I think your grandmother and I can afford both."

"Me, too, Grandpa?"

"You, too, Zeke. That's the whole idea of having you here. We want to help out with things while we can. You won't be living here forever, after all."

"I'd live here forever, Grandpa. It's way cool."

"Way cool?" Grandma said.

"I learnt that from Terell."

"Learned," Jenna and Grandma said at the same time. Then Grandma said, "Now's a good time to learn how to scrub scrambled eggs out of my old black frying pan. Come on, Zeke. We'll have a lesson."

Zeke zeroed in on the messy frying pan with a pot scrubber and bomb sound effects. When he finished scrubbing, he showed the pan to their grandma.

"That's not half bad, Zeke. There're only a couple spots left. I'll just give them a little elbow grease, and we can call that job done."

"Not half bad means pretty good, huh Grandma?" Zeke's T-shirt was wet all down the front.

"It certainly does."

Zeke was so pleased with himself he did a somersault and his feet crashed against the dishwasher, but Grandma said no harm done. Maybe they should get a tumbling mat Zeke could use in the backyard. That's when Jenna figured it out. They were more like a normal family, with adults around for the children.

Jenna took her new journal from the displayed gifts, and ran her fingers over the pressed leaves and flowers on the cover. She'd use it just for special events, like last night's party and soccer camp if she did get to go. The pages had little bumps here and there from leaf and flower parts. She wrote around them, and filled five pages.

Later, when Andi called about soccer camp, Jenna already had the facts. She'd gotten them from Grandpa, who'd gotten them from the Sunday paper. He cut it out with his pocketknife and put it on the refrigerator with a magnet.

Jenna and Andi traded soccer stories over the phone. They talked about mud in their hair and eyes and mouth from slide tackles and scoring on corner kicks and getting carded. Before they hung up, Andi said, "Hey, Jenna, we're going to be friends no matter what the group does."

"I'd like to be friends," Jenna said. But the worry worm had already started crawling around. After she hung up, it crawled faster. How could she be friends with a girl whose dad was a policeman? Well, she decided, she'd just never talk about her dad. She'd talk about how her mom worked and went to school. And about Grandma and Grandpa and how they helped out. Which would work just fine until Andi said, "Why? Why are they helping? Don't you have a dad somewhere?" Jenna was pretty sure Andi would ask. Friends almost always did.

Jenna wrote a *What if* page in her regular journal. *What if* the Snoops did find out her dad was in prison? *What if* they found out that part but not the murder part? *What if* she just said she wasn't allowed to talk about him? *What if* she just forgot all the don't-talk-rules and told the truth?

When her dad called that night, she almost asked him that. *What would happen if I tell my friends you're in prison?* She knew the answer. Her mom would hate her. Instead she talked about the gift he sent.

"Did you carve the top yourself?" She wanted to say, *If you can use sharp tools to carve, why can't you come home?* But she knew better.

"I did, Jenna. I did it in Hobby Shop before I left Monroe. I made three and sold two. It helped pay for the wood, and gave me a little extra to send home to your mom." While she listened, she thought of things she overheard her mom say sometimes. No matter how hard her dad worked, he couldn't make much money. Prison wasn't set up to let men help support their families. Her mom was right; programs and classes didn't put food on the table. From what her dad said next, she wondered if he could read her thoughts through the phone.

"It's a terrible thing for a man to have a family and not support them. There's no way I can ever make that up to you and Zeke and your mom."

"It's okay, Daddy. I think it's better now, being with Grandma and Grandpa." She didn't want her dad to sound so sad. She'd never thought about that part much—that it was hard for him because he couldn't support them. She only thought it was hard because he was locked up and couldn't be with them.

Zeke talked to their dad next, and then their mom shooed them both toward the living room so she could have a private conversation. Jenna and Zeke and their grandpa and grandma were into a Disney movie when their mom got off the phone. She came into the living room with tears running down her face and talked right over the movie's sound.

"I can't believe it. I cannot believe it. Some inmates are all riled up over the Float Incident and they're writing letters to the editor of the *Tribune*. They're using it as a means of bringing attention to what visitors go through. They know the little girl's name and Jenna's, too. Oh, Daddy, what am I going to do now?"

Grandpa found the remote control and turned off the TV and VCR. "Just what you've been doing, I'd think, Lynnie. Hold your head high and carry on, and let the dust settle where it may."

"Will the letters have our names?" Jenna's heart pounded so hard her chest hurt, and she had to push the words past a lump in her throat.

"Mom," Zeke said, as serious as Jenna had ever seen

him, "why come was that a bad thing? When Jenna jumped in the water to save that girl? Was it cuz the girl is black?"

Grandma said, "No, Zeke, that wasn't a bad thing. Not a bad thing at all. It's just that your mom wants to protect you from the stigma of a father in prison."

"Oh." Zeke tipped his head back so he could look at Grandma's eyes. "What's a *stigma?*"

"Why, it's a little like a nasty stain on the carpet when company comes to visit, and they make a point of walking around it. Then after the visit they talk about it to others and avoid coming to visit again."

"That's not nice, huh?"

"No, it's not nice. It's just human nature. We all tend to judge others by the worst we know about them and ignore all the good."

"I know what, Grandma. If we get a nasty stain on the carpet we could put a small rug over it, and then no one would see."

"That's about what we're doing, Zeke," Grandpa said. "Putting a rug over the fact of prison. Trouble is, someone's lifting the corners and peeking under it."

Chapter Fourteen

The first float-incident letter appeared in the paper Friday. Jenna was up in time to watch her grandpa's face when he saw it. And hear his comment. "My sentiments exactly." She'd been a bundle of nerves all week. Every time she'd talked to Andi about soccer camp or the Fourth of July, she'd just wanted to tell and be done with it.

Grandpa handed the paper, folded to quarter size, to Jenna. The letter's headline said MICC Guards Shirk Duty. The letter said, "Lives were put in jeopardy because guards don't care about our families and friends. It's not surprising that another visitor rallied to the rescue before MICC's men and women in blue. Why isn't this incident being investigated?" After the man's name and number, the paper included a note in italics that said the letter was printed with permission of the MICC administration.

"Honest to Pete, why don't they leave well enough alone," Grandma said. "I'll make some scrambled eggs. It seems like a morning that calls for eggs."

Grandpa wiped his glasses on his shirttail.

Jenna tried to hear her grandparents' thoughts. She was pretty sure they were changing the subject. "Will there be more letters do you think? From other inmates? Or the prison?" From her dad with his name and number and italics that said his daughter was the one who rallied to the rescue. He wouldn't say rallied though. He'd say something simpler, like jumped in.

Grandma shrugged. Grandpa said time would tell. Jenna cut out the letter to go with the good Samaritan article. She put the letter and article in the box her dad made, locked it, and hid the key under the mattress.

Saturday's paper left well enough alone. The letters were about safe fireworks and a reminder about a boy who'd lost some fingers the year before. And about Indian reservations, where anyone with money could buy illegal firecrackers. That bothered Jenna. The fact that Indians were allowed by law to sell such things. "Why?" she asked, but it wasn't the time or place. Her mom had to dash off for her weekly visit with Dad and then dash back to work in the afternoon. Grandma needed Jenna to concentrate on getting ready for soccer camp.

"Hurry up, Jenna," Zeke yelled, dragging out her name like an echo. He was more hyper than usual. It took all Grandma's strength to keep him in line.

When they pulled into Howard Park, Grandma said, "You go introduce yourself to your coach, Jenna. I'll see to Zeke. And don't you spend all your time fretting over him. He'll be fine. He's not your responsibility. Isn't that right, Zeke?"

"Uh huh, the onliest reason I can leave my group is to go pee, but I have to say, 'May I use the restroom?' And when we're all through, I'm s'posed to wait right where Grandma dropped us off."

Jenna was looking out the window for Andi, and let onliest go. They got out of the car, and Zeke stood almost still until Grandma came around to take his hand.

"Jenna, you could wait with me, if you want. When it's through. So you won't be alone."

Jenna knew Zeke was nervous. Well, so was she. Then she saw Andi at the edge of the field doing jumping jacks. Andi jumped faster, waved both arms, and ran toward them. "Come on, we're going to kick butt."

Jenna hesitated for a second. "I'll wait afterward with you, Zeke, don't worry."

Their grandma touched Jenna's arm. "You go on now. Let Zeke be. I'll see he ends up where he belongs."

"Come on." Andi tugged her other arm, and Jenna went with her to the sign that said *Girls*.

The morning breeze gave her goose bumps, or maybe it was worrying.

Calm down, calm down, concentrate, concentrate, don't worry about Zeke.

Their group leader, a college girl named Erin, checked Jenna's name on her clipboard. "Let's get to work," Erin said. They dribbled, did touch and go passes, took shots on goal and corner kicks. Erin made them work hard, but she kept saying, "Good work, good work," which made them all work harder. Most of the girls Jenna's age had played on the team Andi's dad helped coach. They called to her by name on passes and gave her high fives. One said, "You've got the moves, girl, what team you on?"

"Uh, I just moved here in April. I played before in Snohomish county." Jenna didn't want to say Monroe, just in case. At Howard Middle, she'd said east of Everett, in case kids could figure it out. If you lived in Monroe, you must be related to someone in prison. If they'd even heard of the town; it was that small.

Someone yelled, "Hey, Andi, get her to try out for our team. We could have one more."

"I'm all over that. She's already met my dad."

Jenna tried to concentrate on what Erin said and not think about teams. Or Andi's dad. Or the fact that try-outs had been in March before Jenna left Monroe.

Then practice was over, and Zeke was with Grandma Randall, who was talking to a tall woman in a long dress. The woman moved, the dress swished, and Jenna saw she wore an ankle bracelet. Andi's mom, Jenna knew, even before Andi ran to her.

"Mama," Andi said, and gave her mother a hug. "This is Jenna. She's way good at soccer. Daddy's going to be psyched. Can I invite her to the Fourth? Did you ask her grandma?"

"Jenna, it is very nice to meet you. I am Kiana Tupou. Andrea, you are soaking wet with sweat. Please save your hugs for after your shower." She sounded stern and looked stern, too, with her hair pulled away from her face and wrapped in a knot at the back of her head. Then she smiled, and her black eyes sparkled, and her face went soft.

"Parents," Andi said. "They never learn. It's Andi, Mom. Can I invite her? What time can we pick her up?"

"We were discussing the Fourth, and I have received Mrs. Randall's permission to include Jenna. We will plan to be at Jenna's house at a quarter before one o'clock, and we will return her at half-past five in the evening."

Andi did her jumping jacks. "We want to stay for the whole day, Mama. Please, please, please."

Mrs. Tupou gave Andi a look; a nice look but firm and final, Jenna thought. Andi must have thought so, too, because she said, "Pooh, well, I tried. See you Monday, Jenna."

On the way home, Zeke rode in the front seat where Grandma could reach over and put a hand on his legs, which bounced even though the rest of him wore a seat belt. Jenna sat in the back seat and thought about Monday. The Fourth of July. She'd be going to Point Defiance Park with a friend. She let their grandma correct Zeke's grammar.

"I'm the best at running. I winned the race every time."

"Won, not winned."

"Yeah, I won, and Kevin said I just need to practice my breathing, and then when we kicked the ball I did it wrong until he showed me, and then I kicked it right, and he said, 'Wow, with that speed and punch we'll put you out at right wing.'"

Jenna leaned forward to pat his shoulder. "That's good, Zeke, that's really good."

Zeke turned and gave her a grin. "Betcha didn't think I could, huh, Jenna?" Then he did something with his voice to sound like their grandpa, and at the same time bopped his head with one fist. "Who'd a thunk it? Thunk, thunk."

"Turn around, Zeke, and sit straight. Remember the rules about riding in the car." Grandma's right hand was on Zeke's shoulder, and her eyes were everywhere at once, including the rearview mirror, where Jenna could see them. "Settle down, now, so we can get home and get some food into you. Something good and heavy to fill those legs of yours and keep your feet on the ground."

Jenna squinted her eyes and looked out the side window. Buildings went by like they were moving and the car was standing still. Thinking did that to her eyes when she was in a car. Worry-thinking, and sorting-thinking, too, it all went together. *Grandma handles Zeke better than Mom. I've always handled Zeke better than Mom does. Mrs. Tupou seems nice. Mr. Tupou is a policeman.*

Jenna thought so hard about that the rest of the way home that she missed Grandma asking what they'd like for lunch, but it wasn't too hard to figure out because Zeke was naming off things. Pizza and hot dogs and Coke and potato chips and Snickers for dessert.

"Well now, let me think. We could put some tomato sauce and bits of ham on an English muffin and top it with some cheese. Would that do for pizza?"

"Yeah, and I could help, huh Grandma? Cuz I'm not half bad. I could make one for Jenna while she takes a shower, cuz Jenna always showers after soccer, but I don't have to cuz I'm a guy. Guys can get away with stinking."

"Not around their grandmas they can't."

"Why come, Grandma?"

Grandma Randall sighed a big sigh, like air escaping from a balloon. "How come, not why come, Zeke. Because Grandmas have more time to pay attention to things like showers and stinking and boys making pizza out of English muffins. I'll get out the ingredients. You get in the shower."

Jenna kept thinking and watching houses roll by until Grandma's rolled up in front of them and stopped. Her brain was stuck on the stigma thing: the part where the wife got treated like a criminal, even though she didn't do a thing wrong. But what about the children? Why did she feel like she was bad? Then she remembered something her dad had told her.

There's a saying, Jenna. "When a parent is in prison, the children waiting at home are doing time, too."

That was it. She was doing time. Waiting for her dad to come home. Waiting to belong to a whole family.

Chapter Fifteen

"Good, you're still up," Jenna's mom said when she got home that night. "I've got some news." She made them wait for the news until after she went to the bathroom and changed into something more comfortable.

When she came back, Zeke said, "And now, The News," with zee sounds on the end like he was already falling asleep.

Grandma smiled. Jenna laughed due to the nerve bundle she seemed to be carrying around. Their mom frowned, but only for a second.

"First, there will be more letters in the paper, but one will be a good one. From Officer Hooper, the woman who saw to Jenna that day. And second…drum roll, please…the officer and the sergeant who were there and some others want to give Jenna a little award the next time she visits. A sort of 'Thank you,' but unofficial."

Jenna's insides jumped. She bit her lips together so she wouldn't ask a dumb question.

Zeke, who liked drum rolls, banged on the coffee table until Grandma took his hands in hers. "Well, now," Grandma said. That meant she was pleased.

Grandpa did a thing with his mouth and nodded. "About time."

The letters, three of them, didn't make it into the paper until Monday. Jenna was caught up in worrying about what to wear for the Fourth of July celebration. Two were inmate complaints about visitor treatment. The third was from C/O Hooper.

As one of the officers present when the child fell from the float, I'd like first to remind all inmates incarcerated at McNeil Island and other state correction facilities that we are corrections officers, not guards. That said, I'd like to remind all concerned that visitors agree to abide by certain rules and expectations. Children under age sixteen must be accompanied by a parent or guardian and monitored by that adult at all times. On the day in question, two officers were assigned to visitors. One was on the float, the other on the dock. Other officers, myself included, had finished our eight-hour shifts in the kitchen or hospital and been replaced at our posts. We were no longer officially on duty. Most of us had been on the island since just after midnight and had boarded the boat. It's safe to say we were anxious to get home. I offer this as explanation, not excuse.

I assisted with the incident, and I know the visitors involved wish to remain anonymous. Please grant them that. Address further concerns through proper channels. Those of you who are inmates know what I mean.

C/O Debra Hooper, Tacoma

Jenna knew her mom liked the part about remaining anonymous. Grandma said she'd hoped it put an end to things. Grandpa said it was time to leave it alone and enjoy the Fourth.

The Fourth of July at Point Defiance Park looked a lot like the state fair in Monroe without animal barns. Popcorn, cotton candy, elephant ears, corn dogs, pizza, Thai food, Cambodian, Mexican, barbecue, burgers, and onions. The air smelled like Grandma's kitchen when she sautéed up a pan of onions for Grandpa's dinner. And like coffee—espresso, latte, cappuccino.

"Yuck," Andi said, "how can people drink that stuff?"

"I like it sometimes," Jenna said. "I like the smell when it's being ground." She and Andi walked behind Lori, Sara, and Kara, who were whispering about something—like they did in school, in homeroom, and the hallways. Jenna hadn't known they were coming until Mrs. Tupou drove up. Sometimes Lori and Sara whispered, and Kara said, "Tell me, tell me, come on you guys." Kara was the extra with Dori away at her real dad's for six weeks.

Andi put a hand on Jenna's arm and whispered. "Sara just got off restriction. I bet she's got plans to meet up with MP. I bet that's what they're talking about."

"Maybe that's why your mom said to check back in one hour," Jenna whispered back. It felt good to be whispering—to be with Andi.

"Watch, they'll try to lose us in the crowd, which I don't even care if they do."

"Oh," Jenna said. It was one of those times where she didn't know the right thing to say. She wouldn't mind those three losing them. She wouldn't mind seeing MP herself, but she wouldn't even think about that. She had enough things to worry about.

"Look, friendship bracelets." Andi headed for an open-sided tent with woven jackets and skirts hanging at the sides and a woman working at a loom in the middle. There was a long table across the front, where two girls about their age made the bracelets. Jenna followed Andi, who picked up a bracelet and studied it on her arm. She put it back with the rest and tried another one. When Jenna looked up, Lori, Sara, and Kara were nowhere to be seen.

"I don't see them. The other three," Jenna said.

"No way am I going to try to keep up with them. It's okay to wear these bracelets during soccer since they're soft. Those three want to find boys. If not MP, then some other boys. Sara doesn't much care. Unless MP's around keeping an eye on her."

"Lori told me she's not into boys. She's into sports. Basketball, anyway."

"Lori says that around Sara because she doesn't like Mexican boys. Lori says they think they're better than blacks. African Americans, I mean. Those two have a love-hate relationship. You know? Lori and Sara? Lori acts like she's the leader of everything, but she follows Sara, and Sara finds the boys. White and black and everything in between, which we are. You and me. Tannish, but not from being in the sun."

"Oh," Jenna said, and wondered what it would be like

to really be part of the group and know all these things. Then she asked Andi the important question. "Do you have a boyfriend?"

"Heck no. Look at me, Jenna. I'm taller and bigger than all the boys I know, except my brother, Luke, and besides, my dad says, 'No boyfriends,' and nobody argues with my dad. My mom says it will take one determined boy to stand up to dad, he looks so tough. He's really a marshmallow inside. You have to get to know him."

"He seemed nice." Jenna's stomach did a little flip. Andi's dad arrested people that committed crimes.

Andi picked up bracelets and put them down. She tipped her head one way then the other. "We could each buy one and exchange. For friendship, you know. How much money did you bring?"

"Twenty dollars." Jenna's grandma gave her two ten-dollar bills and told her to have a good time. Just handed them to her without a lecture about where money came from and how hard it was to come by and warnings about wasting so much as a nickel.

"Better yet, we could make our own. These are expensive. Let's pick something to eat instead. There's every culture here." Andi patted her stomach and counted her money.

"There is? Every culture?"

"Damn near. Oops, sorry. There goes my mouth. I'll be on restriction, next. I know. Let's find Indian fry bread and shave ice. You're Indian so you should have fry bread, and shave ice is a big thing in Hawaii. And I'm pretty sure they don't have any roast pig."

"I saw barbecue ribs."

Andi grinned. It grew into a laugh, and her voice boomed. "I'm talking pig here. The whole pig turning on a pole so its eyes look right at you every time it's head comes up."

People looked at Andi. Jenna smiled, and heard it turn into a laugh. She relaxed. It felt so different from being around Lori and Sara. But maybe she'd be uptight if Andi came to her grandparents' house and asked to see her room. And saw the Polaroid picture on the refrigerator, which Jenna moved to the side where it didn't jump out so much.

"I've never had Indian fry bread. Or shave ice."

"Shave ice? Sure you have. They call them sno-cones here. Or slushies, only they put in more juice and less ice, because it's not always so hot like in Hawaii."

"Sno-cones," said Jenna while she thought about Indian fry bread and all the things she didn't know that Andi did and how she'd ever fit into the Snoops. She'd better be careful or she'd say that name out loud.

Two women ran the fry bread stand. Both had gray mixed into their black hair and more wrinkles than her grandma in their round faces. Their eyes were black. The one who took their money smiled. One of her front teeth was missing, but she didn't seem to care; she looked that happy. She pushed a glass jar toward them.

"Try some jelly. Mountain blueberry, not like blueberry you buy in the market. Go on. Take a clean spoon. Try the jelly then look at the earrings."

They loaded jelly on their fry bread and looked at the

man selling earrings. He sat at a square table covered with beaded things. He had a long braid and a big feather in a black cowboy hat and a leather vest with beaded designs and a round beaded pendant. Earrings dangled from a cardboard stand. Some had little feathers worked in with beads. Some were tiny dream catchers. Trays (which were lids of department store boxes) held hair clips, leather bracelets, and glass vials of tiny beads. Necklaces with pendants like the one he wore hung on a board behind him. The man had black-rimmed glasses with small square glasses sticking out in front of the main ones. He held a threaded needle in his short, thick fingers, and a piece of soft-looking leather with some beads on their way to becoming a design.

The man pushed his glasses down to the full part of his nose, a big round nose on a big round face, and studied them. "Either of you Blood?"

"Blood?"

"She's half, almost half, I'm Pacific Islander. Officially my dad's Samoan; my mom's Hawaiian."

"Close enough. I give you a discount." The man moved his eyes from Andi to Jenna. "You don't know when I say Blood? Your elders not teach you that?"

Jenna swallowed, or tried to, but whatever needed to go down couldn't quite make it. "I don't exactly live with my Indian relatives. My dad's from Canada."

"Your dad don't teach you?"

"I don't exactly live with him, either. Right now I live with my mom and her parents."

"They divorced, huh?"

Jenna thought the man's eyes could see into her head, maybe into her heart to where it hurt. She frowned and looked for a hangnail to pick. Oh boy, now what had she gotten into? "Sort of separated."

"Huh." The man shoved his glasses back in place.

"My dad's an artist. He draws animals and birds and designs like that." Jenna pointed to the man's necklace. "And he carves. Wood. He made a wooden box for my birthday with hummingbirds carved on it."

"Huh." The man dug in his shirt pocket, pulled out a card. It said Indian Traders, and had a picture of a totem pole. "Have him give me a call, I look at his work, maybe we make a deal. I like authentic. Blood, you know what I mean?" He grinned then, and his whole face changed from big, round, and scary-serious to just a nice man trying to sell his work.

"Okay, thanks," Jenna said. How could her dad call? Maybe she could get her dad to send some drawings to her, and she could call. Or take some of his drawings she already had. She could find her way on the bus. But her mom would freak.

Now the man leaned sideways and dug in a pants pocket. "Here, you each take one of these. No charge." He held out narrow strips of leather with a few beads stitched on in elongated diamond patterns. Jenna looked at them, and then at Andi.

"Come on, hold out an arm. I put them on for you. They come with the fry bread, but only for indigenous girls who get a little blueberry jelly on their fingers. Okay?"

Jenna licked off her fingers. People watched. She

Jenna thought the man's eyes could see into her head,
maybe into her heart where it hurt.

glanced at them, then back at the narrow leather bracelet and took in a deep breath and stuck out an arm. At that moment she wanted that strip of leather with the beads that made a long diamond shape as much as she wanted a good friend. The man placed the bracelet on her wrist, touched her hand to turn it palm up, pulled fringes on one end of the leather through a slit on the other end, and shook her arm so the fringes hung down.

"I want to pay something," Jenna said.

"Me, too." Andi had her arm extended toward the man now.

"You already paid something. You want to pay more, come take classes. I teach beading. Culture, too, they go together."

"Me, too?" Andi said again, this time a question. "I already know how to string things. I make shell jewelry."

"Huh," the man said. "You, too."

A voice in the crowd said, "You teach beading? Authentic designs?" Another said, "How much are the earrings?"

Jenna and Andi stepped out of the way. "That's how we paid," Andi whispered. "I bet it is. We got other people interested." Then she boomed, "He teaches beading and culture. You should try the fry bread with blueberry jelly. It's made from real mountain blueberries, not the kind you find at the market."

Jenna looked at the Indian women. One spooned up a dab of blueberry jelly and gave it to a customer to taste. The other wrapped fry bread in a napkin. Jenna looked at the man. One big hand clutched paper money. He raised it and touched the brim of his hat.

"Aloha," Andi said. "That's my word, I don't know yours. Come on, Jenna, it's time to meet my mom. By the way, where does your dad live? I'd like him to meet my dad."

Chapter Sixteen

Jenna felt a chill, though the day was warm. What had her grandma said about answering that question? The one about where her dad lived? She couldn't remember. Her head was filled with a picture of her mom with narrowed eyes and a serious scowl.

"My mom doesn't like me to talk about my dad." She fiddled with the bracelet's leather fringe.

Andi stopped walking. Her eyes had that puzzled look that might as well be big black question marks stamped from brow to cheek.

"It's okay, Jenna, moms are like that. But he's your dad. It seems like you should be able to talk about him. I mean you care about him. It showed in your voice when you said he's an artist."

Jenna took in a deep breath, one meant to give her brain time to think. Instead, her brain thought pizza, barbecue, cinnamon, all at once, and her stomach did a major flip. She tried to swallow and to breathe back out the food smells. Her hand flew up to cover her mouth. Leather fringes dangled from her wrist.

Andi put one hand on Jenna's arm. "Are you going to be sick? I didn't mean to upset you so you'd get sick. You don't have to talk about your parents. Some parents are too much."

"I'm okay. My nose just let in too many food smells at once." Jenna managed a smile. She felt comfortable with Andi. Maybe that wasn't good, either. Maybe it would be better to find other kids whose dads were in prison. Easier. Except her dad didn't necessarily want her to associate with other inmates' families. And her mom would have a fit.

While Jenna was busy in her head, Andi was laughing so hard she had to bend over.

"Your nose let in too many smells? I love it."

Jenna laughed, too. It wasn't that funny, but Andi's laugh got her going.

"We'd better find one of those outhouses. I have to go," Andi said.

"They're called sanicans." Now Jenna couldn't stop laughing.

"Whatever they're called, they still stink, but I need one."

"This way, I think. Come on." Jenna set out through the crowd. Parents yelled at kids who whined; a fat man stuffed half a burrito in his mouth; someone puffed on a cigar.

"Phew," Andi said, "even outhouses smell better than

cigars. They're the worst. We better hurry. I don't want my mom to get mad at us. I can't wait to tell her about our bracelets."

Andi and Jenna were right on time. Lori, Sara, and Kara were ten minutes late. Mrs. Tupou kept looking at her watch. Jenna kept looking at Mrs. Tupou, whose face was round like the women at the fry bread booth, and whose hair and eyebrows and skin were the same brown. Sort of. Like the sergeant on the McNeil Island boat. He'd said something about Native Hawaiian and Native American being alike. They were, and they weren't. It was their hair. The women at the fry bread booth had straight hair. Mrs. Tupou's was pulled back and wound tight, but Jenna knew it had waves in it. Like Andi's.

Mrs. Tupou gave Jenna a puzzled look.

Jenna felt her face get hot. She hadn't meant to stare. She opened her mouth to ask a question, bit her lower lip, and took a breath. She wanted to say she thought Mrs. Tupou was pretty. She wanted to ask what Mrs. Tupou thought about indigenous people. She rolled her lips between her teeth and then unrolled them and opened her mouth. Before she got any words out in the air, she heard Lori shouting and saw her running just ahead of Sara and Kara.

"It's her fault. Sara's; she made us late."

"No way, Lori." Sara stopped beside Lori, pushed her face up to Lori's shoulder, and popped an elbow in her back.

"Yes way, Sara." Lori shoved Sara—just a little shove,

but Sara acted like she was going to fall. Kara caught her shoulders and shook her.

"Please, girls," Mrs. Tupou said. "We're all here now, so let's talk about what we're going to do next."

"Can we go down to the beach? This is, like, boring." Sara dragged out the word.

Mrs. Tupou shook her head. While she was saying "No," Lori said to Andi, "Big surprise. Sara can't find MP. She thinks he might be down at the dock fishing or something."

"Oh, Lori, like you're so perfect. I'm going with Andi and Jenna next time."

"How did you girls get separated?" Mrs. Tupou looked at Sara, but Jenna would have bet she was really asking Andi. She would also bet Andi wouldn't tell, not when they were all there, anyway.

"Well," Sara said and stopped because Lori was talking, too.

"See, they stopped to look at something, and we kept going, and they didn't catch up, and we couldn't find them again."

Andi nodded. "We were looking at friendship bracelets."

"Those look quite smart," Kara said. She left the r out of smart. She sounded very Australian, which she was.

"They aren't real friendship bracelets," Lori said.

Andi made a sound, an impatient huff. "I didn't say they were. I said that's what we stopped to look at. Geez, Lori."

"Girls, that's enough." Mrs. Tupou looked at her watch again.

"Could we, like, have two hours? Before we meet again? I'm not, like, looking for MP, so don't say I am, Lori. It's just hard to see stuff and get back in an hour."

Mrs. Tupou looked each of them in the eye, one at a time. "Meet me right here at four. We'll decide then how to spend our last hour. I'm going to spread out a blanket and read, so you can find me here at any time. And do try to stay together."

They went off, a group of five girls. Jenna felt awkward with them. She didn't exactly know what to say to Andi when the others were there. Not that there was much chance to say anything, because Lori and Sara kept up their spat. Mostly Jenna just listened. Kara wanted a leather bracelet, so Andi led the way. When Lori saw the Indian man she stopped dead in her tracks and planted her hands on her hips.

"Like, now what, Lori?" Sara said.

"No way am I going anywhere near an Indian with a feather. They're worse than Beaners when it comes to prejudice. They hate African Americans."

Kara was already at the table, touching bracelets and talking to the man. She pointed to Andi and Jenna, and the man saluted.

"Oh, come on." Andi gave Lori's arm a tug. "He's really nice."

Lori shoved Andi's hand, and narrowed her eyes. "Don't put your hands on me."

Andi scowled. "You know something, Lori, you're the one that's prejudiced."

Sara called out, "Hey, Geronimo, are you, like, prejudiced against African Americans?"

Kara turned around. Her blue eyes looked big; her face turned red.

Jenna felt her mouth drop open. She covered it before it ran off on its own. Lori hadn't said anything about Indians being prejudiced against blacks before. When she and Sara were in Jenna's room. Or at the skating party. Jenna felt her feet taking her backward away from them, like a hummingbird retreating. She bumped into someone, stepped on a foot, and got pushed.

"Watch it. Watch where you're going. Damn kids." The woman, a fat woman, shoved a second time.

"Sorry, I'm sorry, I didn't mean…" The woman walked away without waiting for Jenna to finish apologizing. Jenna watched after that. Watched as she ran through the crowd. She ran to a line of sanicans, found one that said vacant, and locked herself in. She needed to think. Her stomach contracted. She leaned over the hole, just in case. The stench brought a heave and another. Fry bread and blueberry jelly flew out her mouth. Tears ran down her cheeks. Some throwing-up tears and some sad and lonely tears. She blew her nose, drew in a breath, and gagged again from the smell. She ripped off toilet tissue and held it over her nose and mouth. Over the sound of her own gagging and blowing she heard her name being called. Stretched. She pictured it written like that. Five letters spread clear across the page. Always five letters. Two n's. She'd never be a Snoop; she'd never have a four-letter name. What was it with their talk of being a mixed group? Talk, all talk.

There it was again. Her name, not so long this time, and with a weight at the end. "Jennaaaahh." She pushed the lock up and over, and half stumbled out the door because she forgot about stepping down. Someone pushed past her to get in.

Andi grabbed her shoulders. "There you are, Jenna. I've been yelling my lungs to mush. What happened, girl? Did you get sick?"

Jenna nodded and looked past Andi's broad shoulders for the others. People everywhere. No Lori or Sara or even Kara.

"Look at you. Your eyes are all watery. I'll bet you didn't get sick from the fry bread. I'll bet you got sick from those two mouths. Lori and Sara, they're so uncool. Let's go find my mom."

Jenna shook her head. "No, I'm okay, you go back to them. I'll never be a…" She almost said Snoop. "I'll never be part of the group."

"Yes you will; you have to be. It's the only way to get along at Howard Middle. If you're not part of the group they say bad things about you, and you never have any friends. You never have anybody to hang with. You will be part of the group. It's how you survive." Andi put an arm across Jenna's back.

"They don't really want an Indian. They want a

Hispanic. That's what they thought I was until…until just before my birthday party."

"Hah! You think Lori wants a Hispanic? That's just for Sara's benefit, because of MP, and because she wants to be Sara's friend. Didn't you hear what she said? 'Beaner,' that's what she calls Hispanics."

"Then why do they make such a big deal about how they're a mixed group?"

"For show. It keeps the teachers from coming down on them. Trust me, being part of the Patchwork Quilt…oops, there goes my mouth. Don't tell I told, whatever you do."

"Patchwork Quilt? That's what you're called?" Jenna felt a smile begin. It hadn't tugged at her mouth yet, but it was creeping from her eyes down her cheeks.

"That's what they call us. I just go along. It's really whatever Lori and Sara and Dori and Kara decide. They're the leaders. They can change things at any time. They're the ones who vote you in or out. You have to suck up for a while, Jenna. Jenna? Are you hearing me? It's the only safe thing at Howard. It's protection against the racial gangs. Like that Dorio guy that showed up at the skating rink. They're a Mexican gang, and there're Vietnamese gangs, and Cambodian. You know all that. Right? They're always looking for girls. But they don't mess with girls in the Patchwork Quilt."

Jenna looked at Andi's eyes, black and serious. Beyond Andi she saw Lori, Sara, and Kara coming toward them. "They're right behind you. And don't worry, I'm not going to end up in one of those gangs." *Not a gang and likely not the Patchwork Quilt, either.*

Andi whispered, "Three of the patches, you mean? We'll just say you were really, really sick from something you ate."

"My stomach was just upset for a minute. The smell in the sanican didn't help."

Lori and Sara stopped behind Andi. Kara stopped behind them.

Sara had her hands on her hips. "What, like, happened?" She sounded like a car alarm giving off one screech and stopping at the peak of its high pitch.

"She felt sick to her stomach, and then she got into the sanican, and you know what it looks like in there. You never want to look. You just want to hold your nose and go. But that's not how it works when you need to puke. You have to bend over the hole, right?"

"Gag," Sara said.

"So, you know what happened, and now she wants to just sit down somewhere. We're going to find my mom. Okay? You guys just go ahead and do whatever. Okay?"

Jenna was saying, "You don't need to stay with me," when Andi pinched her elbow and found her funny bone, and her arm jerked.

"Well, okay, if you're sure," Sara said.

"She's sure. She wouldn't say it otherwise," Lori said.

Kara shrugged.

Jenna watched them walk off. "I don't think I can fit. It's not just being part Indian. It's because of my dad. See…" She searched her fingers for a hangnail to bite.

"Here's how I see it, Jenna. Your dad doesn't live with you right now, and he doesn't go to Howard Middle. A year from now it won't matter, because we'll be in high school where there're four times as many kids, and Lori and Sara won't be running anything."

"But…"

"Besides, you can play soccer. You've got the moves. And I already like you better than them, and I want us to be friends. But we need to be part of the group, too. Okay?"

Jenna looked at Andi, who was bigger than seventh grade boys. Well, eighth grade boys; they'd be in eighth now. She was also pretty, but there was something else. Smart about life. What had Grandma Randall said? Smart gets you out of trouble pretty gets you into? Something like that. Andi was smart enough to stop Jenna before she said something that would end their friendship. But the something was still there.

Chapter Seventeen

At soccer camp the next morning, Andi asked Jenna right off how she felt. "Fine," Jenna said, and then it was time for warm-up stretching and running and drills. When their leader called a break, Jenna headed straight for the water cooler. Andi and some girls from the team her policeman-dad helped coach caught up with her.

"Give me five," Andi said, and Jenna raised her hand and slapped Andi's just like she fit right in.

"Me, too," another girl said, and Jenna slapped again. It felt good. Maybe she could try out for the team. If she could keep the whole prison-dad thing quiet. If she didn't let it squirt out. If she could not tell, but not lie, either.

When she'd gotten home the day before, she'd thought about never leaving her grandparents' home again. Grandpa Randall had the barbecue set up in the backyard and chicken ready to go on it. He'd gotten a tumbling mat somewhere and put it right on top of the grass. Zeke was practicing walking on his hands. Grandma had pies in the oven and a potato salad ready with the best ever dressing. She mixed dill pickle juice and mustard in the mayonnaise. The kitchen aroma made Jenna's empty stomach grumble. If it wasn't for soccer camp, she'd have been perfectly happy to stay right there for the rest of the summer. Maybe for the rest of her life. At least all of eighth grade.

Andi grabbed Jenna's hand. "Hey girl, the whistle blew. Toss that cup in the trash and get back to work. We're having a practice game Saturday."

Jenna worked hard and tried not to worry about the *What ifs* she'd written in her journal. She talked with Andi on the phone in the afternoon but only for about ten minutes. Andi's mom had strict rules about phone time, and Grandma Randall did, too. Sort of. She said, "For Pete's sake, Jenna, don't you and Andi get it all said at camp?" That wasn't exactly a rule, but it meant the same.

"We're having a practice game Saturday," Jenna said. "I have to tell Mom I can't go to visiting." She wanted to talk to her dad. Maybe he could make up a good story for her to tell Andi and the others. Not a lie, exactly. Just a reasonable explanation, as Grandma would say.

Her mom actually paid attention when Jenna told her about the practice game.

"We'll go on Sunday. I'll work Saturday. Someone will want to trade. That way you can have your game and still visit and get your award, too."

Grandpa said, "That's a step in the right direction, Lynnie."

Jenna was thinking about adding *step in the right direction* to her journal and almost missed the rest.

"Why not take it a step further and let Zeke stay home. Jenna can talk to her dad and get her award without distraction."

Jenna's mom raised her eyebrows. "That's a thought. We could do that, Jenna, just you and me."

"Distraction," Zeke said, like it was three words set to music, and turned a cartwheel right into Grandpa's legs.

Jenna's mom started the rules and warnings about visiting before they reached the end of the block. Actually, she started them at breakfast, but Grandma made her stop.

"Lynn, can't you see Jenna's already a bundle of nerves, what with seeing her dad and wondering about that award? Honest to Pete, let her eat a little breakfast, or she'll be light-headed from starvation."

But now they were in the car driving away from Grandpa and Grandma Randall's. Just the two of them. The overall rule was, "Do not, under any circumstances, discuss the Float Incident with anyone except the officer who gives you the award. And don't say anything to your dad about the award. It's a surprise for him, too."

"Oh," Jenna said. That gave her a new worry. "So, I can talk to Dad about the Float Incident since that's why I'm going alone with you. And about other things, but not the award. Right?" She bit her tongue; she shouldn't have said *other things* to her mom.

"What other things?"

Jenna looked out the window. The houses were about the same size as her grandparents', but none were as nice. Yards looked messy. In one, grass had grown up around a child's tipped-over riding toy. She wondered what happened to the child. Maybe the mom took the child and left, and the dad didn't care anymore.

"Jenna, I asked you a question. What *things*? I hope you don't mean what I said that one time about *divorce*."

Jenna turned to look at her mom, who was looking at her and back at the street and then back at her again. "I mean about his art and stuff like that." She hadn't told her mom or grandparents about Indian Traders or the Indian man. She hadn't even showed her mom the beaded leather bracelet. It was stored in her box with the Float Incident news clippings. "About being allowed to carve." She'd gotten it in her mind that he could make some money by carving things to sell.

Her mom, who didn't know that part, groaned. "I explained about Hobby Shop. About checking out tools, and how nobody leaves until all the tools are checked back in."

Jenna watched her mom take in a breath that lifted her shoulders. She saw the look that meant she'd better pay attention.

"Inmates do every kind of work imaginable in prison. That's how the place runs. You know that. They handle all kinds of tools and equipment. A little carving tool is not a big deal, Jenna. Your dad is not the type who's going to run around stabbing people with a little carving tool."

Jenna rolled her lips between her teeth and bit. She needed to think before she spoke so she'd say it right. Her mom signaled for a turn and muttered something about a driver who wasn't paying attention.

"I know that, Mom, about inmates doing the work and Dad not being dangerous. It's just that with his art…" Jenna paused for a second to organize her words about selling his art, and her mom butted right in.

"His art is a hobby, Jenna. That's why it's called Hobby Shop. I'd like to have time for a hobby."

Jenna gave up. She'd wait until they were with her dad. When they turned into the parking lot at the bus depot, she said, "Mom, do you still love Dad?"

"Oh, for God's sake, Jenna. What do you think this is all about? Putting myself through all this crap to visit? Do you think I'd visit someone I didn't love?" Her mom pulled into a parking slot and turned off the engine. "Now, remember, not one word about the Float Incident. If anyone on the bus or in the dock house says anything to you, do not answer. Let me handle it. If the officer at the dock is the same one, do not even make eye contact with him. Or with any other visitors. Just keep your eyes down and your mouth shut."

"Do you want me to walk several paces behind, too?" Jenna asked. Her mom was way ahead and didn't hear, which was probably a good thing. Jenna knew better than to be sarcastic.

Two corrections officers boarded the bus, but they

didn't look familiar. The bus driver had a brimmed cap pulled low over dark glasses and chewed gum with his mouth open. She was pretty sure he didn't recognize her. Most of the passengers were young children with women of all ages. Some must be mothers of inmates. Not many men visited. Maybe inmates didn't have dads, which might be why they got in trouble in the first place.

On their way from the bus to the dock, Jenna drifted into her *What ifs*. *What if* the officer that checked them in said something? *What if* he looked at her name and shook his head and wouldn't let her board the boat? What would her mom do then? Jenna imagined herself left alone to wander around Steilacoom while her mom visited. She wouldn't mind; she would like to see the town. She was still imagining when her mom gave her a little tug, and they were through the scanner and in the waiting room. Then they were on the boat with twenty minutes until they docked on the other side. At the float where the whole thing started.

"Do not even look at the spot where you jumped in," Jenna's mom said when the boat slowed down. "Thank goodness the dock officer was different than that day. Thank goodness that woman and all those kids aren't visiting today. Thank goodness the tide's high."

Jenna nodded and went into her journal mind where she wrote an essay about Dads in Prison. Maybe she'd turn it into a Letter to the Editor. *Dear Editor*, she would write, *My dad is in prison for killing another man. He's an inmate, but he's still a dad. He said one time that children*

of inmates are doing time, too, waiting for their parents to
come home. That is true. For instance, I am not allowed to
tell anyone about my dad, or where he is, which is hard.
How can I make new friends when I can't tell? And if I did
tell, would they still be my friends? My mom says inmates'
wives get treated like criminals, even though they didn't do
anything wrong. Well, so do inmates' children, but I can't
tell my mom that.

Jenna left her journal mind and looked at her mom. Why couldn't she tell her mom? The inmate crew who handled the ramp and ropes jumped onto the float. She didn't have much time. She put her hand on her mother's arm to get her attention. "Mom?"

"What, Jenna? I know you're nervous, but just keep your mouth shut and your eyes down. And stay in line. Especially stay in line. Just remember the rules, and everything will be okay."

That's why she couldn't tell her mom. They didn't speak the same language. Jenna sighed, but not too loud. "Okay," she said, and followed her mom down the ramp onto the float. An officer stood at the float's edge where the little girl had fallen in.

"Good," Jenna whispered into the salty breeze.

Chapter Eighteen

When Jenna's dad hugged her he said, "I'm proud of you for risking your life for the little girl. Proud with a capital P." Jenna had her eyes squeezed shut, but tears snuck out and ran down her cheeks. Her dad wiped them off with his thumbs. She knew a corrections officer watched, but she didn't care. She didn't even care about her mom's impatient sighs.

Then her dad and mom kissed and hugged, and her mom whispered something that Jenna knew wasn't "I love you." For one thing it was too many words. More likely her mom said, "Watch what you say about the Float Incident, and don't let her get into Other Things."

Jenna told her dad the whole Float Incident story the way it happened. Sometimes she had to back up because she remembered a part she'd skipped. Her mom interrupted a lot. Twice her dad said, "Lynn, let Jenna finish." And twice, when her mom said other inmates were watching, he said, "Don't worry about it."

Of course her mom worried. Jenna could tell by the

way she sat. When Jenna switched to the birthday party, her mom relaxed. Her dad said, "Tell me more about that, Jenna," a hundred times. Well, five at least. And about soccer camp, when she switched to that. He said other things, too. Like, "I can tell you had fun," about the party and, "It makes you feel good," about soccer.

"Zeke feels good about soccer, too," Jenna said. "His coach says he's got a great foot, and he's the fastest boy in his age group, and..." She stopped because her mom squeezed her arm, and there stood Sergeant Kanahele and Officer Hooper. Her dad's eyes narrowed. He pushed his chair back and stood.

"May we join you?" Sergeant Kanahele asked. "We have something for Jenna."

"Yes, of course," Jenna's dad said. The men shook hands, and then everybody shook hands and said names, and Jenna worried because her palms felt sweaty. Then all the adults talked at once. Finally, they all sat down.

"We won't stay long," the sergeant said.

"Just long enough to give Jenna an award," Officer Hooper said.

"An award?" Jenna's dad said. His eyes narrowed again.

"A good Samaritan award from the sarge and me and a few others. I call it our You-Go-Girl award. We got permission from headquarters, but we still have to keep it on the QT." She handed Jenna an envelope that had Nordstrom printed in the return address corner. "Go on, open it."

Now Jenna's hands were sweaty and shaky both. She

pulled out a gift certificate. With her name on it. For one hundred dollars. There was a thank-you card, too, but she couldn't read it because her eyes were all wet and her nose was running.

"That's so you can get yourself some new shoes," Officer Hooper said. "Or whatever you'd like." She patted Jenna's hand. "You're an amazing young woman, you know that?"

Jenna managed to say thanks. So did her dad and mom. They said other things, too, but she didn't really hear. Everybody stood up and shook hands again, and Sergeant Kanahele and Officer Hooper said they had to get back to their posts.

"Wow!" Jenna's dad said. "I can't believe it."

"Neither can I," her mom said. "A hundred dollars. At Nordstrom's. I've never had a hundred dollars to spend just on myself."

"Now, Lynn…"

"Don't start, Bernie. I'm going to the restroom."

Jenna's dad leaned back in his chair. He looked tired. "I'm sorry your mom reacted like that," he said.

"It's okay. Mom worries about money. I can share the gift certificate with her." Her dad started to protest. She interrupted, and talked fast. "I want to ask something while Mom's gone. What should I tell my friends about you? When they ask? That's reasonable, but doesn't mention prison? And that's not a lie?"

"Phew," her dad said. His forehead wrinkled and his eyes scrunched. Then he answered one of his Dad answers that would have had her mom groaning. "It's hard to have a dad in prison. It makes you feel ashamed."

"Oh, no," she said, though she was. Ashamed.

"Jenna, it's okay to feel that. It's normal. The shame belongs to me, but it got placed on you. On all the family. Shame is the thing that makes you feel like something about you is wrong. That you're less than other girls your age because your dad's in prison. Is that how you feel?"

Jenna let her head nod—just a little. She needed her dad's help. She wanted a dad who was proud of her all the time. She wanted a dad she could be proud of back. With a capital P. And she wanted a friend, just one real friend. When she looked up, Jenna saw her handsome dad through a blur caused by her wet eyes. Handsome doesn't look so good when the person inside feels sad. Which her dad felt; she could tell.

"Oh, Daddy, I don't really care about those Snoops." She leaned against his shoulder. He patted her back. It wasn't exactly a hug, which would have been against visiting rules, but it was close enough to one to upset her mom who came back just then.

"Jenna, sit up! Bernie, for God's sake, what are you thinking?"

Jenna sat up so fast she rocked the chair. It sounded like Zeke was there. Her dad stood, took her mom's hands, and helped her sit. He moved their chairs close together so they sat with Jenna in the middle. He spoke just above a whisper, but his words came through like he shouted from across the room.

"Lynn, we're going to talk about some things. The three of us. It's time."

Jenna's mom groaned and leaned forward so far her hair swept the table. A little tic pulled at the outside corner of her dad's right eye. He talked across Jenna but to her at the same time.

"The Don't Tell rule isn't working for Jenna. She's thirteen and on her way to being an independent person. She has her own needs and feelings. She has to decide what works for her in her independent world."

Her mom's head whipped up. Her eyes looked frozen, they were that cold.

"You're not the one out there, Bernie. You don't know what it's like."

"No, I don't, but I do know some truths. Maybe I learned more from books than from being there, but the books aren't all wrong."

Now her dad's eyes were hard, too. Jenna couldn't stand it. She looked at her dad and then her mom. "It's okay; the Don't Tell rule's okay. I'll just keep saying Dad's away. I won't tell anybody."

Her dad looked right into her eyes. "Jenna, the point is you need to decide what to tell based on your own feelings, not on your mom's rule."

"Bernie, I'm warning you."

Her dad looked at her mom. His right eye twitched. "Lynn, I love you, and I love our children. And I believe you'll all be relieved when the truth is out."

Jenna's mom pushed away from the table. "What do

you want me to do? Call the paper and tell them the whole story? The good Samaritan of the Float Incident was Jenna MacDonald, daughter of Bernie MacDonald. Bernie has a psychology degree and knows all about being a parent. However, he's in prison for murder."

Jenna tried to grab her mom's hands. "Mom."

Her dad sat very still, his hands open and flat on the table. "We're not talking about that incident. We're talking about shame. We're talking about a prison that's harder to survive than this one where I live."

Lynn's eyes narrowed and her nostrils flared. "You're right about that, Bernie. It's easier to be here than out there. A job. School. Two kids, one of them hyper."

Jenna felt numb. Novocain numb when it starts to wear off. Her lips tingled; even her hair tingled. She had to say something to stop her parents before it was too late. "Zeke's better since we're with Grandma and Grandpa. It helps. They help with money, too, Mom. They said that's the whole idea—to make it easier for you."

A corrections officer walked by. Jenna's dad kept his voice soft and low. His eyes stayed sad.

"I wanted your mom to take you to your grandparents' a long time ago, Jenna. I wanted you to settle there when you were young and get established there. But I wanted your mom to visit me, too. We decided she'd buy the trailer in Monroe so she and I could stay close. So I could see you and then Zeke, too, when he came along. I know now it was selfish. I was selfish. It was too hard for your mom."

The Don't Tell rule isn't working for Jenna.

Jenna's mom said, "You said you'd never have to do this much time, Bernie. You said you'd appeal…get your time reduced…"

"I believed I would, Lynn. My attorney believed I would. But we were wrong."

"So all of a sudden we're going to announce who we are to the world. I'll be that inmate's wife. Jenna and Zeke will be that inmate's kids. Is that what you want?"

Jenna's dad drew in a deep breath. "I want to help Jenna. I want her to let go of shame that belongs to me. I want Jenna to tell her own truths."

"And what about me? What happens to me when Jenna goes around letting go of her shame? Telling her own truths? That's all I want to know, Bernie. What…about…me?"

Jenna's dad took in a deep breath. "You're an adult, Lynn. You get to choose. No one but you can decide whether to deal with it or keep on hiding. You use your paralegal program as a reason to hide the truth. They can't deny you an opportunity because of me. You are not a criminal, Lynn, and you need to stop acting like you are." One hand went up to cover his eyes. A few seconds later, his fingers and thumb wiped his closed lids.

Jenna was searching for a way to comfort them both when her mom leaned in front of her. "It's all well and good for you to talk about denial and shame, Bernie. It doesn't cause you any problems to say, 'You're free to tell your own truths, Jenna.' But let me tell you, it's not that easy. Jenna will get judged. She'll never have friends if people know."

"Mom, please."

"Don't Mom, please me, Jenna. Do you think those girls would go to a skating party with a criminal's daughter? Or invite a criminal's daughter to play on their soccer team?"

Jenna closed her eyes. Why didn't her mom know that's exactly what worried her? Her mom slapped the table. Her dad said, "Easy, Lynn," and took one of her hands and one of Jenna's.

Veins in Lynn's neck bulged from shouting without raising her voice. "Answer me, Jenna. Do you think they'll want you for a friend when you go around telling your truths?"

"I don't know, Mom. I don't know what they'll do. I guess I don't really expect to have friends. Or to be on a soccer team with Andi."

"Well you should think about that. You should think very hard about that."

"That's about all I've been doing. Ever since we moved to Tacoma." Jenna's dad tightened his hold on her hand, but he didn't interrupt. She kept her head turned toward her mom. "I don't like saying, 'My dad's away.' 'My dad doesn't live with us.' Kids just ask the next question, and the next one. 'Are your parents divorced?' 'Where does he live?' 'Do you, like, visit on weekends and stuff?' What am I supposed to say when they ask?"

"Why can't you just say, 'I don't want to talk about my dad?' What's so hard about saying that?"

Jenna looked at her dad. He nodded his head. "You can answer that, Jenna."

"What's so hard is it's not true. It's not true, Mom. I do want to talk about him." Jenna heard tears in her voice.

"Fine, Jenna, you talk. You choose to tell, and you're choosing for Zeke and me, too. Do you think that's fair?"

"What's fair about any of this, Mom? What's fair?"

Chapter Nineteen

Jenna's mom spent most of the drive home saying, "Think about it, Jenna. Think hard." Jenna spent most of it wiping away tears. She wanted to get to her room without being noticed by Grandma and Grandpa. It didn't work. Grandma looked up from her magazine.

"Now what happened?"

Jenna's mom was hot on her heels, as Grandma would say. "I'll tell you what happened. Bernie gave Jenna permission to *tell her own truths*. That's what happened."

"Oh, for Pete's sake," Grandma said.

Grandpa turned off the ball game. "Well, it's about time. Peel off the scab. Let out the pus."

Zeke turned a somersault on the living room floor. "Puusssss. Oooooze."

Lynn groaned.

Jenna said, "I'm going to my room."

She flopped on her bed, her mind busy thinking about what her dad had said. She was thirteen. She could tell her own truths. If she chose.

After a few minutes she got out her journal and wrote about the visit. She was crying again and had to blow her nose about a hundred times. She didn't want to make her mom mad or to hurt Zeke; she just didn't want to lie. She turned to a clean page and wrote the Letter to the Editor she'd written in her mind on the boat ride to the island.

Dear Editor: My dad is in prison for killing another man. He's an inmate, but he's still a dad…

It helped to get that truth on paper, though she would never send it to the editor. For now, just her journal would know.

When soccer camp ended, Zeke started swimming lessons, and Jenna went along to watch. Lori's brother Terell was in the same group, so Grandma and Mrs. Johnson took turns driving. Jenna saw Lori twice and imagined asking her how she really felt about Indians. Then she'd ask how Lori felt about criminals. Then she'd say, *Well, my dad is both.* Of course she didn't. Lori was not the person she intended to tell first.

She wanted to tell Andi, but for once her mouth stayed shut. She needed to spend more time thinking. It was only fair. Grandma said her mom was on pins and needles and told Jenna not to be in a hurry to let the cat out of the bag. Zeke said, "I'm keeping my lips zipped, cuz Grandma said." Only Grandpa seemed to think it was time to open the window and let in some fresh air.

Jenna added those sayings to her regular journal. She wrote them in a letter to her dad, too, and told him about

Indian Traders. She tried to write a letter about feelings, but words didn't exactly work. Grandma was right. She was a bundle of nerves and a bubble ready to burst.

The next week Jenna started advanced swimming lessons, and Andi left for two weeks in Hawaii. Lori and Sara came by one afternoon when Jenna was at the Y being evaluated for Junior Lifesaving lessons. It was easier than being evaluated for the Patchwork Quilt. Lori and Sara left a note written by Sara. It said, *I hope your having a really fun summer.* Jenna changed *your* to *you're*, and put the note in her journal.

The last Sunday in July the *News Tribune* local section had a feature story about the little girl who fell off the McNeil Island float. The picture showed two girls holding hands, just like they did on the visit. The boy that Grandpa said looked Indian was sitting on a riding toy. The mother held the baby.

Grandpa read the article first. Then Grandma read it. "I tell you," she said, and handed the paper to Jenna. The story said Vanessa, the little girl who fell from the float, would like to thank the big girl that jumped in after her, but the Department of Corrections personnel weren't releasing her name. When Jenna's mom read the article, she said, "Thank God."

The next afternoon Jenna had the house to herself; Grandma had taken Zeke for a quick trip to the grocery store. Jenna was in her room with news clippings spread out on her bed and her journals open. She was staring at the window, thinking about what to say in a letter to her dad and saw eyes staring back. Sara's eyes.

Sara knocked on the window. "Hey, Jenna."

Jenna had about two seconds to decide what to do: clean up the mess or run upstairs. "I'll be right up," she yelled to the window. "Meet me on the porch." She found her sandals. Wrong feet. Tried again, ran up the steps, across the kitchen, and through the living room.

Sara plopped into a porch chair. "I'm, like, way bored. Lori's at basketball camp, and MP has to work for his dad. They have, like, a business. Yard care. Can you believe it? MP pulls weeds and stuff. It makes his hands icky. Sometimes he runs lawn mowers. Big deal."

Jenna's heart was trying to jump out her ears. "Oh, Lori's at basketball camp." That's why Sara was there by herself.

"And Kara's on vacation."

"Andi is, too. On vacation. In Hawaii."

"Yeah, I know. But Andi's not, like, one of my very best friends. Lori is, and Kara, and Rika after Lori, and then Dori, who's gone for the entire summer because of her dad." Sara took the clip out of her hair and shook her head. Hair fell across one eye. She took a handful and put the ends in her mouth.

"Oh." Jenna wished she could think of something to say. All she could think was, *Good, I'm glad Andi's not one of your best friends.*

"So, what are you doing? You were, like, not here last week when me and Lori came over."

Lori and I, Jenna almost said. "Swimming. Junior Lifesaving class at the Y."

"Are you going to, like, get a job at a pool?"

"Maybe. I might help teach beginning swimming." Jenna looked at her hands. She needed a hangnail to nibble.

Sara stood up like she was getting ready to leave. "Come on, let's go down to your room."

Jenna jumped up. "My room's a mess." She tried to block the door, but Sara got to it first.

"It's okay," Sara said and went into the house ahead of Jenna. "I need to, like, fix my hair. I'll use your mirror."

Jenna protested in her mind. She bit her lips, opened the door to the basement, and went ahead of Sara. She opened her bedroom door. The box her dad made was open on her desk. She just needed to get the newspaper clippings gathered up and into it. And lock it. Where was the key?

"Just a minute. I'll shovel this stuff off my bed." Jenna swept papers together. They were all different sizes and didn't sweep up very well. She didn't want to wrinkle them.

"Like, what is all that stuff?"

"Just some news articles I'm saving." Jenna walked to her desk on legs gone weak. Jell-O legs like the time Sara looked at the picture on the refrigerator. *Get the articles in the box, close the lid, lock it. Where's the key?* Her hands shook. She put the clippings in the box, shoved at loose edges, closed the lid, and heard the little click of the latch. *Key. Where's the key?*

Sara was beside her, running fingers over the carved hummingbirds. "This is way cool. Let me see the inside."

"It's just plain."

"I want to see, Jenna."

Sara had her hands on the box, on the lock release button. It popped open. Jenna stopped the lid. Sara grabbed the box bottom. Jenna held the lid. Sara tugged. Jenna heard a squeak silent as a mouse, loud as thunder as a tiny nail pulled out of wood.

"Put it down, Sara, it's private."

The second Jenna said "private," she wanted to bite off her tongue and lock it up somewhere. Sara's eyes walked up Jenna's front.

"Private? Like a secret?" Sara's eyes walked back to the box. "Nothing's private when we're, like, evaluating you." She gave the box a little shove and walked away.

Jenna looked at the loose hinge on the back of the box. Her hands shook, but she managed to push the little nail back into wood. It looked okay. Key? She fished in her shorts pocket, found the key, locked the box, dropped the key back into her pocket, and turned around. Sara was stomach down on the bed with Jenna's open journals.

Jenna froze. "That's private, too."

Sara's eyes came up from the page and looked at Jenna. "Gol, is this, like, true? This thing that says 'Dear Editor, My dad's in prison? For killing somebody?'"

Cold swept over Jenna, leaving her numb. "Give me the journal, Sara."

Sara held the journal out of reach. Hair fell across her face. Her hair clip was on the bed beside her. "Your dad's in prison? That's why you live with your grandparents? Huh? Huh, Jenna?"

"Just give me the journal." Jenna's heart thumped back

to life. It thudded so hard she didn't recognize her own voice.

"Here, take it." Sara threw the journal onto the floor. It skittered on the tiles and bumped a desk leg. "Wait 'til Lori hears. You'll be toast at Howard Middle, Jenna."

Sara was gone before Jenna could reply. Jenna heard her bedroom door slam, heard Sara's feet on the stairs, heard the door to the kitchen open and close, and then the screen door. Through her high window she watched Sara's feet and legs disappear. She picked up her journal. Sara's hair clip sat open on her bed.

Chapter Twenty

That night after dinner Grandpa said, "Come on, we're going for a ride." Grandma grabbed her purse and a sweater. That meant Grandma knew what Grandpa was up to. Jenna had told them everything about Sara and the Snoops who were really the Patchwork Quilt. She told her mom, too. Her mom said, "Well, I hope you're happy." After that, her mom didn't talk to her.

Zeke asked, "Are we going out for ice cream? Cuz we didn't get no dessert."

"We didn't get any dessert, Zeke," Jenna said.

"That's what I said, Jenna. You were off in your thoughts, huh? Grandma says you're off in your thoughts a lot these days."

Grandpa said, "Get some ice cream on the way home. First we're going to a little park with a big swing. Glider swing that grandparents can sit on with their grandchildren."

They crossed the freeway and headed in the direction her mom took when they went to visit her dad. They wound around and finally turned onto a road with evergreen trees and maples and a narrow bridge across a creek.

Grandpa said, "Back way to Steilacoom. Nice little town. Old Indian settlement. Fort for a time. Lot more things than just the place the McNeil Island ferry docks." He poked through town so they could look at the buildings. When he turned right toward the water he said, "Restaurant there on the left sells old-fashioned sodas. Restaurant here on the right used to be a lumberman's home. Some folks say a ghost lives there. A good ghost. Straight ahead's the swing."

Jenna sat next to her grandpa on the swing. Zeke, who was busy making ghost noises, sat next to Grandma. While Grandma and Zeke talked about ghosts, Grandpa talked just to Jenna.

"That's where your dad lives for now. Right across there. All in all, not such a terrible place. Puget Sound out front. Good view of Mount Rainier on a clear day."

Jenna stood up so she could see better. She looked across the Sound at the island. It was mostly green with a cleared area where the buildings stood. The ferry was halfway between the island and Steilacoom. A breeze blew a clean, salty smell to her nostrils. She could hear laughter from the restaurant and smell food. Cars went by. Zeke jumped off the swing. Grandma followed him. They went toward an outdoor stage. Jenna's grandpa took her hand.

"I'm not so good with words, Jenna. Likely not so good

even as you. I want you to know your dad's a good man who did a bad thing. He's in prison for the bad thing, but he's still your dad. He didn't have an easy life, being taken away from his people and adopted out."

"Why did that happen? Why did he get…taken away."

"Lots of alcohol problems in those Canadian tribes. In all Indian tribes, really. That's no excuse; it's just a fact. Folks that took those kids from the reservations thought they were doing right. The important thing is your dad survived and he studied and he sorted it out. From what your mom says, I'm guessing he wants you to do your own sorting now."

Jenna's stomach cramped. She bent forward to ease the pain. "Do you like my dad, Grandpa?"

"I like him well enough. Wasn't all that pleased when your mom married him. Then you were born, and it didn't matter so much. Don't much like what prison does to a man's children. Or the wife."

"I know. It's been hard for Mom."

"Yes. Yes, it has. But it's her job to help her children cope. I don't think your mom's been doing that part of her job very well. That's why I wanted to bring you down here. You're free, Jenna. Free to do your sorting, free to visit Steilacoom and look across the water. Free to speak out when you're ready. Free to switch from Howard Middle to another school if you like. Your grandma and I will handle your mom."

"Thanks, Grandpa. I'll probably make it through

That's where your dad lives now. All in all, not such a terrible place.

another year at Howard." Jenna put her arms around her grandpa's neck and hugged. And sniffed, because her nose was running. Her eyes, too. Grandpa hugged back and patted. He kept patting even though Zeke called her name.

"Look, Jenna, look. In that upstairs window. See the curtain waving out the window? See it?"

"I see it, Zeke."

He lowered his voice. "It's the ghost waving to us. And Jenna, you know why come it's waving? It's cuz it's time to tell the truths. Grandma said. For our mom, too. Huh, Grandma?"

"That's right, Zeke. I'm going to help your mom with that."

When her grandma called Jenna to the phone a couple of days later, she knew it would be Andi. She took the phone and closed her eyes so they wouldn't go into squirt-bottle mode. It had been a tense two days with Grandma and Mom going the rounds. That's what her grandpa called it.

"Hello?"

"Jenna, girl, it's Andi. I just got home last night. Sara is so uncool, I'm out of the Patchwork Quilt. They're a bunch of jerks. I can't stand them. My dad wants to talk to you. He's on the other phone."

Before Jenna could say a word, she heard Andi's dad's voice.

"Hello, Jenna. This is Mano Tupou."

Jenna whispered, "Hello, Mr. Tupou."

"First, I want to tell you how sorry I am to learn about your father. That must be very difficult for you."

"Yes." She couldn't stop the squirt bottle. Tears ran down her cheeks.

"I had an uncle that spent some time in jail. That was back in Samoa. It was hard for the entire family."

"Yes. I mean, I'm sure it was."

"Next thing, I'm not suggesting the girls' group at Howard Middle School is a gang, but I'd prefer Andrea didn't belong."

"Daddy, you said I was out of the group and that was that."

Mr. Tupou chuckled. "I did say that, Jenna, but Andrea had already told her mother and me she didn't want anything more to do with them. Not as a group, at any rate."

"I don't," Andi said. "Not since the Fourth of July. I've been thinking about it ever since. Sara's the worst. When they voted on me, she's the one who voted no, but the others voted yes."

"Oh." Jenna didn't know what to say. She'd have to write in her journal to find out what she felt.

"Now tell her about soccer practice, Daddy."

Mr. Tupou laughed. "I've heard a lot about your skills, Jenna. We'd like you to practice with our team, if your mother and grandparents agree. We will be practicing Tuesday and Thursday evenings at Howard Park. Five to six-thirty. I know that interferes with dinner schedules."

Jenna smiled and she sniffed a hundred times to stop

the tears. Well, twice. "I'm sure it's okay. My grandparents want me to play soccer and swim and stuff like that."

"Good. I look forward to seeing you on the soccer field tomorrow evening."

"Thanks, Mr. Tupou."

"Don't hang up, don't hang up," Andi said. "We've got to talk. We're going to be close friends, Jenna, I can tell."

They talked for an hour. Neither Grandma nor Grandpa said a word about being on the phone too long. Afterward, Jenna wrote two words in her journal: *prison* and *free*. After each she wrote thoughts that wandered into feelings. Her dad was more free than her mom because of their choices.

The next morning, Mrs. Johnson dropped by out of the blue. That's how Grandma described it later. Terrell and Rydell, with Zeke leading, ran to the backyard to tumble on the mat Grandpa got Zeke. Grandma put on the kettle for tea. Mrs. Johnson grabbed Jenna like she was ready to skate and gave her a hug.

"I'm sorry about Sara's meanness, and I'm sorry your dad is in prison. Life is too darn hard for you kids these days. Lori and my boys have to cope with biracial issues that are no more their fault than your dad's situation is your fault. Am I making any sense?"

Jenna nodded. She tried to smile, but it was too hard because her face muscles scrunched up for crying.

"Good," Mrs. Johnson said, "because Lori has me about convinced I'm not making any sense at all. I've been on a rampage about that secret club she's in with

Sara…that Patchwork thing. I told Lori either the club disbands immediately or there's no basketball. I had no idea what they were up to. When Lori's father heard, he said he'd see to it the club disbanded, and he called the school principal."

Mrs. Johnson took two sips of tea and a bite of cookie and turned to Jenna's grandma. "Do you think that's wrong of us, Jean?"

"Not at all, Sandy. That's part of being a parent."

Mrs. Johnson sighed. "Lori said she'd never forgive me. Who would have thought it would be such hard work?"

Grandma sighed, too. "Who would think I'd still be trying to sort out my daughter when she's in her thirties and a mother herself?"

"Are you having any success?" Mrs. Johnson asked.

"I'm seeing some signs," Grandma said.

Jenna wrote the whole conversation in her journal and added her thoughts. *Kids who want to have secret clubs will have them even if parents and teachers and principals say they can't.*

By the end of soccer practice the next night Jenna's right hand stung from high fives. It was a select team. She and Andi were the only girls from Howard Middle. Half the girls lived outside the Tacoma city limits. One lived in Steilacoom. Jenna and Andi gathered up practice cones and talked about a Labor Day tournament in Yakima. Which was in eastern Washington. It would be Jenna's first trip across the Cascade Mountains. If she made the team.

"You're on the team, girl. Catch a clue. My dad's stoked, and so's the other coach." Andi looked at Jenna. And then past her. And frowned. "Damn, here comes MP. What do you suppose he wants?"

"Hey, Andi. Hey, Jenna."

"Hey back, MP." Andi's eyes were in question mark mode.

"Hi," Jenna said. She shivered.

"Jenna, could I ask you something?" He glanced at Andi and back. "It's kinda private."

Andi's hands closed into fists and landed on her hips. "If Sara sent you…"

"Sara don't know nothin' about this."

Jenna took in a breath. "If it's about my dad, you can ask in front of Andi. She's my friend; she knows everything."

"She does?" MP looked at Jenna, at Andi, back at Jenna, then at his feet. "It's about my dad. My real dad. See, I live with my mom and stepdad, and…well…I just wondered what it's like. McNeil Island. See, my real dad's there. But I can't visit."

"Why not?" Andi asked. Her fists still rested on her hips.

"Kids underage need an approved adult with them," Jenna said. She looked at MP, so handsome and so sad.

"No way is my mom or stepdad gonna take me." He touched Jenna's hand, pulled his back, put it in his pocket, and pushed grass around with his toe. "I'm not asking to go along with you and your grandparents…"

"She goes with her mom, MP."

MP looked at Andi. "Oh." He looked at Jenna. "Or your mom. I just want to talk to someone who knows what it's about. You know what I'm saying?"

Jenna nodded. "I know, MP, but I don't think Sara would like that."

"Me and Sara broke up. You way cool, Jenna. And smart, too, huh?"

Andi whooped and started doing jumping jacks. Jenna smiled. She couldn't help it. "We can talk MP, but you might not think I'm way cool for long. I'll start correcting your grammar like I do my little brother's."

Mr. Tupou's voice boomed across the field. "Andrea? Jenna? You girls ready?"

"We're ready, Daddy," Andi called. Then to Jenna she said, "I give up. He'll never call me Andi."

MP said, "That's okay by me, Jenna. If you correct my grammar. Mostly I talk like that for show. You know what I'm saying?"

Jenna nodded. She did know. "Okay, then, we can talk. I'll ask my mom about taking you with us if the prison approves it."

"So, that means I can call you? Tomorrow maybe?"

Those little bonfires were back in MP's eyes. Jenna couldn't find her breath. She nodded. Andi grabbed her hand. They ran across the field.

"It's a good thing you're going to be busy with soccer,"

Andi said. "Otherwise MP would start taking up all your time."

"Not my close-friend's time with you, Andi." MP might steal her breath for a minute, but Andi gave it back. And made her feel good about herself. The other night on the phone, Andi had said they were more alike than they were different.

Andi stopped running. "Give me five, girl."

Jenna almost tripped. She felt a laugh coming up from deep inside. It rippled across the field. "I can't, Andi. You're holding my high-five hand."

OTHER BOOKS BY JAN WALKER

Dancing to the Concertina's Tune: A prison teacher's memoir, Northeastern University Press (Boston) 2004.

Parenting From a Distance: Your rights and responsibilities, The Interstate Publishers (Danville, IL) 1987, reissued by Book Publishers Network 2005.

Absaroka: Where the Anguish of a Soldier Meets the Land of the Crow
by Joan Bochmann

In this heartfelt drama of love, war, and the tenacity of the human spirit, young Matt Reed returns from Vietnam to find his Wyoming ranch stripped of livestock, his mother gone, a victim of cancer, and his father a mere shadow of his former self. Will Matt allow an old rival to ravage the ranch with strip mining? Jill, a lovely neighbor; Joe, a Crow Indian friend; and a wild horse herd each play a part in the solution—and Matt's healing.

Danny's Dragon, a Story of Wartime Loss
by Janet Muirhead Hill (coming summer, 2006)

A young boy from a Montana cattle ranch and his family suffer the loss of a father in the Iraq war and grieve as they deal with the emotional, physical, and financial effects of their loss. You will empathize with Danny, his sister, and mother as they learn to adjust their lives—and their thinking.

To order, please contact:
Raven Publishing, P.O. Box 2866, Norris, MT 59745

Or phone 406-685-3545; toll free 866-685-3545

Or visit us on the web at www.ravenpublishing.net
email: info@ravenpublishing.net